Fatal Attack

A Gripping Suspense Thriller

Teagan Stone Series
Book 9

Ava S. King

304 Publishing Company

Disclaimer

A work of fiction contains strong language and explicit content and is only intended for mature readers. The story may contain unconventional situations, language, and sexual encounters that may offend some readers. This book is for mature readers (18+).

Latest Releases: Ava S. King

Agent Red Series

Fatal Memory Teagan Stone Book 1

Fatal Target Teagan Stone Book 2

Fatal Crime Teagan Stone Book 3

Fatal Justice Teagan Stone Book 4

Fatal Enemy Teagan Stone Book 5

Fatal Death Teagan Stone Book 6

Fatal Revenge Teagan Stone Book 7

Fatal Pursuit Teagan Stone Book 8

Fatal Attack Teagan Stone Book 9

Fatal Mission Teagan Stone Book 10

Jessica Smith Series

Mirror of Lies -A Jessica Smith Book 1

Mirror of Lust -A Jessica Smith Book 2

Mirror Of Danger -A Jessica Smith Book 3

Upcoming Releases

Christina Harris- Thriller, Suspense Book 1

Agent Red Fatal Mission Teagan Stone Book 10

Restored: Andi Easton Book 2

Introduction

Sign-up to Ava S. King's mailing list for news, new releases and special offers.

www.authoravasking.com

Synopsis

Today she can be your doctor, tomorrow your neighbor. This spy knows how to blend in and how to save the world.

Teagan Stone has mastered the art of being a spy. She blends into the background, going unseen until she needs to step out of the darkness to save the world.

Running an elite undercover team around the world to prevent terrorism attacks, her work is never acknowledged. But the fact that you're safe at night is a testimony to the work Teagan and her team does every day.

When there is threat made for an attack on US soil, Teagan and her team jump into action to save the world once again, but this time a ripple effect might neutralize their efforts and thousands of lives could be lost.

Will Teagan be able to fight terrorism again or will this be the first time she fails?

Chapter One

It was a quiet day after a whole week of rain. Angela Balman looked at those little kids running about the park. She smiled, thinking of those carefree and happy days when there was no judgment and no worries of the world. She gulped down the water in her bottle as she stopped at a bench near the edge of the park.

She glanced down at her watch and was immediately annoyed. She knew the day was going to drag. As a nine-one-one operator, listening to calls and hearing those voices unraveled her nerves at first, but over time she has managed to control the stress and anxiety it brought.

Angela walked across to toss her empty water bottle in the trash. Then she strolled over to her car, pressed the key to disarm the alarm and climbed inside. She took a moment to scroll her emails and seeing nothing important, she turned the ignition and let the air conditioner blast cool air on her heated skin. She closed her eyes and took a moment to enjoy it.

Upon climbing in, she turned on the ignition, pressed

the air conditioner and closed her eyes to enjoy the cool air.

Ring, Ring

Grumbling under her breath, she reached to answer her phone.

Angela reached with her left hand to pull the seatbelt forward across her waist. "Hello." She glanced to the right, to the left, then the rearview mirror before putting the car in reverse.

"Don't hang up," a deep robotic voice pierced through the phone.

She removed the phone from her ear in confusion. "What?" Angela asked.

"Angela, if you hang up this phone I will blow up the U.S. Capitol building," the strange voice continued to speak.

Angela giggled. It was too early in the day to play pranks on her phone. "Stacey, are you drunk?" Thinking one of her friends was playing a trick on her, Angela shook her head and put her car in reverse. Thoughts of the time Stacy tried to set her up on a blind date replayed in her mind.

"Angela Balman, thirty years old, single living alone. Mariel Balman, your mother on dialysis living in Wisconsin, travels a few times a year to visit. Father dead."

Something was wrong at the mention of her parents. The hairs on the back of her neck stood up as chills ran down her back. A friend wouldn't do a prank that includes mention of her sick mother and the death of her father. Her brows rose in shock. Angela frantically looked around the park because she wanted to know where the call was coming from.

Fear and *uneasiness* crept into her voice. "Who is this?"

"Glad to have your attention."

She reversed out of the parking lot, pulling out the phone and placing it on speakerphone. "If this is a prank, you will be in huge trouble!" Angela yelled.

"Did you get your workout in this morning, Angela?" the robotic tone taunted.

Angela gasped and then stammered, "Ho-How do you know where I am?"

"Be waiting for my next call," the caller warned and hung up.

Angela felt like her blissful happy, mundane workday would be boring and uneventful and now in a split second that blissful, happy feeling was gone. Her eyes rapidly searched the area to see if she noticed any man or teenagers playing on the phone. Nowadays you couldn't be sure with AI technology that people weren't roaming around pranking folks just to get a rise out of them. Angela rushed to dial one of her girlfriends as she sat stunned in her car.

"Hey, Angie," Constance answered.

Her hands clinched the steering wheel. "Constance, are you at home?"

"I am. Are you okay?"

Angela pulled away from Constitution Gardens Park and headed toward Main Street to get home safely. The loud screeching of tires pushed her to jump in nervousness as they approached the red light. An older woman next to her flipped off the young boys in the jeep up front.

Angela took deep breaths and rubbed her chest. "I had the strangest phone call."

"What kind of a call?"

Suddenly, Angela noticed a man at the corner of the light pole staring at her holding a newspaper.

"Some guy-"

"Angela, you there?"

"Constance, I think I'm being followed."

Constance laughed. "Huh, have you been drinking early this morning?" They have been longtime friends, and they were college roommates.

Angela worked as a schoolteacher while Constance worked for an investment firm. They would get together monthly for drinks with a few other friends to catch up on their lives, and they usually worked out together in the morning, but today, Constance couldn't make it because of an emergency at work.

Angela pressed the gas and flew through the green light when all of a sudden, a bus ran a red light on her right side. The collision made time go in slow motion as everything went black. Seconds later blood dripped down her face, as smoke spilled from the engine, and a horn blasted in the air. Her blonde hair matted to her head from the collision. Blood continued to spill down her forehead, and dark bruises started to appear on her arm and legs. Some people rerouted and parked to jump from their cars to help. A few rushed from the sidewalk to see if she was alive. Sadly others brought out their phones to record the scene to put on the internet.

Constance screamed through the phone. "Angela! Angela!"

There were people screaming. The bus driver was bent over the wheel with a head injury as passengers explained help was coming.

A traffic jam started to pile up in the area as the ambulance and police sirens blasted in the air, letting people know help was close. The same tall figure with short black spiky hair and thin mustache who stood near the light holding a newspaper approached her car. He stared at her unconscious body for a few moments, smiled then strolled back to his car to leave.

* * *

A few blocks over from the car crash, Emily Rose, a college student, walked alongside the bus stop while she listened to her playlist on her phone and texted.

She stood near the route five sign in the direction of Rice University and bobbed her head to the beat. Someone bumped into her shoulder and she removed her headphones. Heat flushed through her cheeks in aggravation.

Emily shifted her backpack on her shoulder and angrily tossed her hair into a high bun. "Hey, watch where you're going, man!" she shouted and flexed her hand.

Ring!

Emily grumbled and answered the phone as she glanced at the time, noticing the bus was running ten minutes late. Normally her bus was early.

She flung her hands out, then picked up the call. "I need a car. The bus always takes forever," she said into her device.

"Emily Rose," a raspy voice spoke.

She bit her fingernail and made a mental note to get a manicure appointment. "This is Emily."

"Emily, are you heading to school at Rice University?"

Emily reared her head back in surprise that someone knew what school she attended. "Who is speaking?"

"A bomb is going to go off at the U.S. Capitol building in two days."

Emily chuckled at the statement. "What? Bryan, I swear you have to stop playing on my phone. I told you we can't hook up this weekend because I have upcoming tests I need to study for." Bryan was a close friend who she'd met months back in her senior year at Rice on campus at a party. He'd become a situationship but she'd slowly started liking him and hoping it would become a relationship. Her red pouty lips poked out, and her hand planted on her hip.

"You have less than one hour to stop it."

She twisted a string of hair around her finger. "First off, I am heading to class and Bryan, you know I have a test in twenty minutes."

"This is not Bryan. Emily, you're going to watch people die if you hang up and not do as we say."

Emily tensed up at his words.

Struck breathless, she panicked with anxiety. "You are not joking."

"The reason your bus is late is because of a car accident that happened ten minutes earlier. Are you listening to your favorite playlist of Ariana Grande?"

The comment Emily heard made her eyes bulge wide and she started walking backwards toward her apartment, scanning the area for help.

"Don't move."

She froze.

"I-I," she stammered, as her body shook and her eyes filled with tears.

"Going somewhere?" the same robotic voice Angela received a call from questioned.

Her belly became a sinking stone at the stranger on the phone knowing her exact whereabouts. "Please. I can't help you."

The voice laughed on the other end of the call. "You have one minute after this call to contact this number and tell them to be at this address in ten minutes."

"Wait a minute-"

He disconnected the call and a second later a phone number she didn't recognize appeared in her message app along with the address to the U.S. Capitol back entrance.

Thick with the sorrow of people dying, Emily peered around, hands shaking, a sudden thirst torturing her throat at the threatening call about blowing up a building, let alone the U.S. Capitol and killing people. Emily shifted and ran back to her apartment a few blocks away from the school. She jogged up the stairs, pulling her keys out of her pocket while looking over her shoulder. After hearing the door slam, she fell back against the wall in the hallway and clasped a hand around her mouth in nervousness.

Her neighbor, Josh's, brows stabbed high in confusion. "Hey, Emily, are you alright?" He cautiously approached with a hand out to help her stand.

A fog of heaviness breached into her mind. She rested a hand on her forehead. "Why do you ask?"

His gaze bounced from her to the ground and up to her face. "You look like you were scared about something."

Emily bent down to pick up her keys, then turned her back to him. "I'm fine. I-I need to get inside."

Josh waved goodbye as she shoved the door closed and

headed to the elevator to leave. "Emily, what are you doing back so fast?" Rubina her roommate came out of the bedroom into the living room holding books in her hand, and her coat on her shoulder. They'd lived together since their freshmen year. Rubina was the one who helped Emily get used to how things went on campus and helped her get a job at the library. Both ladies were around twenty-two and the only child of their parents, and both were studying to become nurses.

Emily rushed past and Rubina trailed her into the kitchen. Emily opened the fridge and grabbed a bottle of water. "Rubina, I need your help."

Emily twisted the top off and gulped it down. Rubina watched her with concern as Emily grabbed another bottle. She pursed her lips together.

Rubina lifted the top and sipped before putting it on the counter. "Are you okay? You seem a little freaked out."

Emily drew air in and out of her nose, held her phone up to her face and tapped the screen. "This." Slowly it began to sink in that this was a serious situation and she was caught up in some strange web of terror.

"Your phone." Rubina smiled.

Emily shook her head. "Read the message."

Rubina took the phone out of her hand and scanned the message. "A phone number and address to the U.S. Capitol."

"He wants to blow up the U.S. Capitol."

Rubina chuckled and handed the phone back to her, then walked around and headed back to the living room.

Emily gripped Rubina by the elbow to stop her from leaving. Rubina's brows knitted in confusion at Emily's jumpy demeanor.

Flabbergasted, Emily tossed her arms up in the air. "Rubina, it is serious. I was getting ready to get on the bus when I got a phone call."

"Okay, we always get spam callers."

"No, this one was different. I think he's following me or something." The steady strum of her heartbeat caused her to feel sharp pains, and she rubbed a hand over her chest.

"Who?"

"That's what I don't know. He said something about a car accident that caused the bus to run late today."

Rubina shrugged and bent down to grab her things. "May be some kids playing on your phone."

"We need to go to the police."

Rubina trekked to the door, then turned the knob and cracked it open. "Emily, I have a class later on, plus my date with Joseph."

"He said-"

Rubina held up her hand. "Look, I know you've been stressed with school lately. Maybe taking a vacation this weekend to your parents would help."

Emily slouched down on the couch and stared down at her phone. "Yeah, a vacation could help."

"Call me later!" Rubina yelled, closing the door behind her.

Ring!

A mysterious call appeared on Emily's screen and she tossed the phone. While shaking with anxiety, Emily pushed off the couch, picked up the phone and clicked to accept the call. In a whisper, she said, "Hello."

"Emily, where are you?"

"Morgan."

"Duh, who else is your best friend?" Morgan giggled.

Emily closed and opened her eyes, blew out a breath and laughed. "Sorry, I thought you were someone else for a minute." Feeling relief she raked a hand down her face, and sat up on the chair.

"Well, it is me. So are we still meeting before class?"

"Uhm...I..."

"What are you doing?"

"I have to tell you something, but I don't want you to think I'm crazy."

"Try me."

"I went to get -"

Knock, Knock!

"Emily," Morgan called her name.

Emily stood up and ambled to the door. "Wait, someone's at the door." Without looking she pulled it open to find a letter on the ground. Emily stuck her head out into the hallway seeing the elevators close up.

"Emily, are you there?"

Her features twisted into a maddening glare. "Morgan someone left a note and walked away."

"A note?"

Emily bent down and picked it up to see her name across the front. "Well, a letter I guess."

"What's strange about that?" Morgan was one of her closest friends since being in college. Often times she'd had to go to her for support whenever she had tension with her parents about how strict they were with paying for her college and controlling her choices.

Emily slipped the letter from the envelope and headed back to her chair, reading the words U.S. Capitol in bold font. She threw it to the ground like a flame; a raised alert of panic trickled up her spine. All the color drained from her face.

"Oh my god!"

"Emily! Are you alright?"

As she shook with clenched stomach muscles and rigid posture, she felt lightheaded and collapsed on the floor. In a whisper, she spoke into the phone. "Morgan..."

The quiet normal day that Angela and Emily were used to had transformed with one phone call that had changed their lives forever. It was the same words that would haunt them forever from the dark, twisted edginess in the tone of what was demanded of them to do. It was enough to give anyone the sense of being unable to control all forces around them.

Chapter Two

Director Teagan Stone listened to one of her latest crime podcasts on the drive to the hospital to bring lunch to one of her friends. She only had a few briefs lined up for the day, and a call from her Team Lead, Spider, that she could take from home later today without going into the office.

"Call from home," the Bluetooth voice interrupted the podcast.

"Boss, are you staying here for a while?" Jason her driver interrupted her as she took the call. He pulled into the parking entrance to let her out.

Teagan lifted the phone and stared as Spider's name scrolled across the screen. "About thirty-forty minutes." Upon clicking the green button, she grabbed the tacos she knew Jamila would enjoy and her purse and climbed out of the car. Jason placed the car in park, turned the radio low and sat back prepared to wait.

Teagan adjusted her jacket sleeve. "Spider, you rang."

"Are you going to need me sitting in on the meeting?"

Teagan looked at her watch. "I will. We're going over

the budget for the team, so I want to make sure we're not completely cutting ourselves short."

Boom!

The sudden thrust of the blast sent Teagan in the air a few feet off the ground. It jolted Jason in the car. A loud car alarm roamed in the air. People along the sidewalk shouted and screamed at the large flames, and fire floated in the sky.

"Teagan! Teagan!" Spider yelled.

Teagan slowly opened her eyes. People ran back and forth, trying to help anyone hurt. Teagan gently turned over on her back. She raised her hand up to her forehead, blinked her eyes and patted her chest, checking her body for injuries.

Against her better judgement, she tried to stand. "Jason...Ughhh," she moaned, then paused for a moment as if hesitant about her next thought.

"Ma'am, are you alright?" A security guard approached and reached for her hand to check her pulse. Teagan lifted a leg to stand up.

"Maybe you should wait for the doctor to check you before standing."

"Jason. Where is Jason?"

Teagan scanned the hospital parking lot. "What happened? I can stand."

He pointed at the smoke and fire in the air. "Something blew up over there."

Teagan's eyes followed his hand in the air and saw the smoke and heard the wail of sirens as ambulances drove in that direction.

She peeled off her jacket, patting her pants pocket. "Shit. Where's my phone?"

"Teagan! We have to go!" Jason called out. He bolted

from the car and rushed toward her.

A wave of grayness passed over her. She reached down to grab her things. "I need my phone and shit. Jamila."

He held his phone up for her to take. "Call her on the way back to the office. I got Spider on the phone."

Teagan swiped it from his hand, sprinted back to the vehicle, and scanned the area of people all in disbelief at what was going on in front of their faces.

"Are you good?" Spider questioned.

Teagan snatched the seatbelt over her chest, tossed her purse to the side, and shoved her jacket to the floor. "I'm fine. I need answers on what just happened."

"Shit," Spider hissed.

"What? Spider, talk to me!"

A pile of cars creeped down the road, driving slow to see the smoke and flames. Jason honked the horn for them to move.

"We got the red phone."

Jason placed the car in reverse, maneuvered backwards to the other side of the hospital exit, then pulled out of the parking entrance, speeding down the road.

"Get us to the Agency! Fuck speed limits!" Teagan shouted and disconnected the call with Spider. Teagan dialed her husband's number.

"Hey, babe," Christian answered.

"Christian. Christian. Are you home?" Teagan's stomach sagged in dread.

"I took the kids to the park."

Teagan's breath picked up. "We have a red phone."

"Teagan, are you safe? Where are you?"

Normally, giving out details was forbidden, but Teagan ran by her own rules as the Director of the

Agency. After she informed him years ago that the red phone was the alarm of a terrorist attack, she trained him on getting the kids packed and sent to the office for protection.

She looked to Jason, then back down to her phone and placed the call on speaker. "How far out are we?"

"About ten minutes," he responded.

"We're ten minutes away."

"Okay, I love you. Stay safe."

A group of people rushed down the street holding a pile of clothes and merchandise.

"You too. Keep them calm."

"Are we sure it's not a false alarm?" Christian probed.

Teagan scanned her dirty clothes and the scars on her hands. "It's not a false alarm."

Right as Jason was about to turn left, a car came out of nowhere and blocked them from moving forward.

"Something's wrong," Teagan muttered.

"Babe, are you good?"

Teagan clicked back over to talk to Spider, her heart picked up speed, and she knew the amount of distractions happening at once only meant something bigger was set to go off.

Jason looked out of the window. "Shit, they're backed up for a few blocks."

"Spider, we are held up. Make sure the team is briefed. I will get there soon. Do we know what got hit?"

"A few news reports are running that it was a bus," Spider replied.

Teagan bit her bottom lip. "Alright keep me posted. I have to make a call to the president."

"Copy that. Be careful," Spider responded.

Teagan blew out a breath and went back to her husband. "Christian."

"I know. We're in the car and heading to you now."

Teagan scrubbed a hand down her cheek. "I love you." Teagan gestured to Jason to look at the trail of police cars rushing through the light.

"Love you more and the kids are good."

"You're the best."

Teagan and Christian had plans to celebrate their anniversary this year with just the two of them going on a trip together. Their kids were good and the family in good health.

Finally traffic was moving. Teagan hung up and pointed to the nearby trail of people standing nearby the area of the blast.

Her features drew tight. A deep furrow got tangled in her brow. "Pull over here."

"I thought you wanted to get to the office."

"We will, but I want to go and see what's happening first."

He eased to the right, put the car in park near the curve and Teagan jumped out and sprinted around the slow cars and moved through the crowd.

"Teagan, hold up!" Jason yelled.

She held her hand out to pause traffic and ran further up ahead. "Is anyone hurt?"

A few people shook their heads. "I'm not sure. I came out of the coffee shop across the street and saw people running," a younger man wearing an apron, holding a bag of food explained.

Teagan watched a few policemen direct cars through the opposite direction.

The young man raked a hand through his dreadlocks

and shook his head. "This happening a few blocks from the Capitol is crazy."

Teagan looked up at him, then down the street in the direction of the Capitol and the White House. "A few blocks," she mumbled.

"Everybody please stand back!" a policeman shouted.

Teagan stepped away from the crowd and spoke with the cop. "Can you tell me if anyone was hurt?"

"Ma'am, that's confidential information."

She reached for her badge on her hip and realized it was back in the car. "I'm with the -"

He cut her off with a wave of his hand. "Don't care. We need everyone to stay back."

"Sir, I left my ID in my car, but I can promise I am with law enforcement."

He covered his eyes from the sun and squinted down at her. "Everyone says that."

Teagan rolled her eyes and turned to head back to her vehicle pissed at not getting nearer the accident.

"Did he say anything?"

"No, he won't let me in since I don't have ID."

"Are you going to lock down the area?"

Ring!

Teagan stared at her phone with an unknown private number and answered. "Mr. President."

He sighed. "Agent Red."

"I know."

"We can't have a panic in the public."

"I know. They're still securing the area."

"Is your team on the way?"

Teagan peered around the streets, watching more cars pass by. "I tried to get closer, but a few police officers aren't letting me in to see anything. I know we have divisions that will take over, but I have a feeling something else is coming."

"Do whatever you need to get this handled. We can't have more bombs going off in DC. I have to get something to the public," the president spoke.

"Understood."

Her driver poked her on the arm and pointed to the right. "Teagan, look over there."

A line of black SUVs driving in blocked off more streets.

"I think it's too late."

"What do you-"

"FBI is here."

The president sighed. "Let me make some calls."

"I'm going to head to the office to find out what's going on." Teagan ended the call and dropped the phone in her pocket.

Teagan climbed in the front seat, shut the door and pulled her seatbelt over her chest. She watched the men in FBI gear speak with the local police.

After returning to the Agency twenty minutes later, Teagan rushed down the hall to her office, used her badge to push forward and entered to find her children watching television and husband reading the newspaper.

"Mommy!" Tatum, the youngest child, leaped up from the couch and ran into her arms.

Teagan kissed her on top of the forehead. "Hey, baby."

"We had fun at the park."

She grabbed a hold of her braids and ran a hand down her arm. "Did you ride on the swing?"

Christian laid the newspaper on the tabletop and

stood from his seat. He walked toward them, gripped Teagan's hand and kissed the back of it.

"Mom, how long do we have to stay here?" CJ wondered, throwing his basketball in the air.

Teagan looked from Christian back to her son and smiled. "Not long, baby. I need to check in with my team."

"Okay, can we have pizza for dinner?" CJ asked.

"I don't see why not."

Christian grasped her hand. "Guys, stay here. I need to talk to your mom really quick." Christian led Teagan from the office and into the hallway.

Christian folded his arms. "Any news?"

Teagan cut the distance in between them, placed her head on his chest and wrapped her arms around his waist. "No, I think it's best if you and the kids stay here."

"You know they'll start fussing, Teagan."

Spider jogged down the hall holding a piece of paper in the air. "Teagan, glad you're here."

Christian and Teagan just stared at each other. Spider froze at the tension.

"Can I talk to him really quick?" Teagan asked.

"Do what you do best." Christian pressed a kiss to her forehead, walked around them and went back in with the kids.

Teagan grabbed the paper and trekked into the conference room with a large crew of people talking and yelling over each other.

"Hold up!" Spider shouted.

Daughtrey fixed his eyes on her. "Teagan, finally. What the fuck is going on out there?" Daughtrey demanded.

"We don't know."

Spider plopped down in the chair next to her.

The whiteboard in the corner held pictures and notes of the current updates, a projector played traffic details from the bus explosion.

Teagan stood in front of the room. "I spoke with the president about getting us access to the area."

Daughtrey tossed a ball in his hand. "What about us taking it over from the FBI?"

Teagan bit her bottom lip and brushed a hand through her hair. "That's the goal, but you know how things play out when we go in and take over."

From the angle of the smoke and flames, it couldn't be mistaken that the bomb was set on purpose.

"So far the only casualty is the bus driver," Spider explained, reading over his text messages.

Gregory turned around in his seat and pointed to his computer. "I was able to log into the camera footage from that cross street."

Teagan sat up in her seat. "Tell me something good."

"No one is shown going on the bus besides the driver. They stepped out at the change point and hopped on from the other person."

Teagan looked at Daughtrey. "Do we have names yet?"

Daughtrey typed on his cell phone. "Coming in hot."

The projector changed to show the bus drivers that were on for the day for the route.

Teagan pointed at the screen and sat on the edge of the conference table. "Get me everything you know on them."

"On it now."

"Spider, push harder on getting us access, if you have some contacts at the FBI."

"You got it, T."

Teagan clapped her hands together to get everyone's attention. "You know like me we are not leaving tonight, so call your families and make sure everybody is secure and protected. Until we know more, this is priority over anything else."

Everyone nodded their heads.

"Good, let's get to work." Teagan walked to the whiteboard and read over the notes, felt her phone vibrating and saw Jamila calling.

"Jamila, I am so sorry."

"I heard about what happened and knew you were on your way here to visit," Jamila said.

Teagan faced the window and drew her lower lip between her teeth. "Sorry, I was going to call you sooner but got caught up here. Plus, trying to make sure the kids and Christian are good."

A TV screen in the corner showed the latest reports and people still crowding the area. Gregory continued typing on the computer. Another team member laid out blueprints on the table marking up the blast points.

"I am just glad you're all safe. The hospital is overloaded with patients. I will be here for another day or two and then head home."

"Glad to hear, and you got a ride home?"

"Montel is here, won't leave my side." Jamila giggled, mentioning her boyfriend.

"Happy everything went okay. Keep me updated on the physical therapy with your leg."

"I will. Talk to you soon and be careful, T."

"Always." She ended the call and faced the TV screen in a daze. Then she peered into the shaggy ridges of the trees lined along the side street of the building.

Gregory's face collapsed into a complex of wrinkles. "Teagan."

"Yeah."

Peace and quiet was a must for her to sort out her thoughts, arrange them, and impose order in battling a new enemy.

"We got to be ten steps ahead if they're planning something else."

Teagan strolled toward him and slipped her phone in her pocket. "I know."

He looked up into her face. "You ready for this again?"

Teagan and Gregory walked out of the conference room and back to her office door and she took a deep breath before answering his question.

"No, but I have no choice but to get ready."

"No other choice."

Their unique quality and experience helped to keep the world in working order day and night without a thank you or an award. No one was driven by ego, or yielded to the impulse to see a better future.

Chapter Three

An hour before the explosion Kenny Thompson laughed along with his coworker about the pre-game season of the football team. He'd bet a hundred bucks for the hometown team and won and planned on taking his wife out for date night. Kenny pulled the car around and stopped near his usual spot close to H Street, waiting to take over the route. He closed out of the phone call, having listened to his wife talk about the latest gossip with her church friends.

"Have a good day, honey."

"Love you, Marie."

"Love you more, Kenny."

He smiled, slipped the phone in his pocket and pushed the door open. He watched the bus arrive behind the company car and picked up his bag. Kenny walked to the door, then exchanged words with Antonio, the driver that was ready to head home.

"How's she moving?" Kenny checked.

Antonio clapped him on the shoulder. "No problems today, Kenny boy."

Kenny shut the door behind him and placed his bag behind his seat. He pushed the visor to the side to block out the sun.

Finally checking all of the side mirrors, he bent down to toss the trash and noticed a picture of Antonio and a baby in his arms. Kenny smiled, grabbed the picture and started to get off the bus when he saw Antonio drive off.

"I'll give it to him later."

Kenny sat down in the chair, slipped the key in and turned the ignition on. As he pulled into traffic, he smelled a weird gas. Right as he started to pull over to the side, the bus exploded, shattering glass from local businesses on the street and shaking the foundation underneath.

Teagan clicked the rewind button on the remote. She watched the footage over and over all night while Christian and the kids slept in the family room to give her space to work. She sat in her office studying the briefing that was updated every hour by the team.

Knock, Knock!

Teagan stretched her arms wide and placed a hand over her mouth to cover a yawn. "Come in." She shuffled papers away.

Christian stepped into her office, still wearing the clothes from earlier in the day. "Hey, kids are asleep."

"Hey. You can't sleep?"

Christian cocked his head to the side. "I was worried about you."

Teagan smiled and dropped the iPad on the desk, stood and walked to meet Christian in the middle of the room.

"How mad are the kids?"

"Not mad at all since the family room is basically an

arcade to them." Christian chuckled and placed a hand on her lower back.

Teagan trailed Christian to the couch. "The Agency built it for people with kids in mind and wanted to make it as comfortable as possible."

Christian ran a hand down her cheek and cupped the back of her neck. "You need to sleep."

Teagan leaned her hand on his shoulder. "I will as soon as we get more information."

The silence, compared to outside her office, emitted her whole body to intense fear.

"Have you eaten?"

"I had a sandwich."

Christian raked a hand down over her shoulder, down to her arm and to her leg. "You think another attack will happen." For all of the years they've been married, Christian's never held this much worry in his voice. Teagan knew her normally reserved and stoic husband would be undone if something happened to his family.

Knock, Knock!

Teagan rose from the couch and sauntered to the door. "Any news?"

"We got clearance," Daughtrey answered.

Teagan whipped her head around at her husband. "I have to go."

Christian sat forward. "Be safe." A sudden unspeakable quiet communication passed between the couple.

"As soon as I know anything you can take the kids home."

Christian smiled. "Yes, Agent Red."

Teagan smirked and moved to the desk. She snatched up her badge, gun, and holster, leaving her office to her husband. Daughtrey, Gregory, and Spider met her at the elevator as the doors pinged open.

"What time is it?"

Daughtrey raised his wrist to check the time. "Nine pm."

All four crowded in together.

Gregory pressed the ground level button. "They've cleaned everything up probably." Spider lifted his cell phone reading over the latest news of the explosion.

"The President will give us full rights over the scene, but make sure we have all the needed paperwork."

As the elevator dinged and the doors opened, all of the team trailed behind Teagan. Gregory headed to the cage on the right, unlocked and removed vests, then passed guns to each team member to stock up.

Teagan popped the back passenger side open, hopped in the backseat and pulled her badge over her head. Daughtrey slid in the driver's seat, Spider in the front passenger, and Gregory in the back. The gates widened for more vehicles and started to drive out onto the street, waiting for Teagan's team to lead the route to the main road to H Street.

Feeling her phone vibrating in her pocket, Teagan pulled out her phone and scrolled to see a message from her husband.

Christian: *Be careful, babe.*
Teagan: *I won't be long, have to check the scene.*

Normally going to a scene wouldn't last long, Christian knew to expect her at a reasonable time, but something in her wanted to be transparent as things started to move closer to becoming a major hit on a big city.

Daughtrey turned on the radio channel listening to the latest reports as people went on about their business as normal for the day. Spider talked on the phone, giving directions to other team members.

Gregory nudged Teagan on the arm to look up as the car came to a stop at the light. To her left she noticed a few people holding signs in their hands.

"Time for US to suffer!" a man with short spiky hair shouted and threw his fist in the air.

Gregory pointed his finger at the tall man in all black and a short beard. "Look at that one."

"Only the beginning until you learn what we've gone through."

"Fight for Freedom!" the entire group of people yelled.

Spider raised his phone and took a picture of the signs and the people.

"Run facial recognitions and police reports ASAP," Teagan demanded.

Gregory typed on his MacBook Air. "What if they were out here when it happened?"

"It would be foolish to be out here right after it happened, but Spider, I need someone on them."

Daughtrey swerved around the corner and pulled to the side of the road. Spider jumped out. Gregory rolled the window down and Spider passed his phone to him and pulled his hoodie over his head.

"Get back in touch if you find anything out, or get in touch with the police if it becomes a problem," Teagan commanded.

"Gregory, get those photos ran and have a car pick me up in four hours," Spider ordered.

"On it," Gregory responded.

Daughtrey pushed forward down the alley and

arrived minutes later at the location of the bombing. The FBI was still on location as more reporters were stationed further behind barriers. Teagan climbed out of the car and motioned for Daughtrey to follow alongside her. Gregory stood next to the truck.

"You know they might be pissed right."

Teagan raised her hair into a ponytail, and pulled her shades out to cover her eyes. "Already know when we come through it will be a problem."

Daughtrey stuck his hand out and held up his badge. "Gentlemen, we got word the scene is going to be transferring over to us. Warren, how is it looking?"

The cold stare and pinched brows of Warren, with his bulky FBI vest, wearing black trim shades and a mustache, took them in and he snarled at them. "Only reason you got the scene is because of kissing ass with the president."

Teagan propped her hands on her hips. "Warren, how many times will you act like a baby against my team?" she accused him in a frigid voice.

"Fuck you. We all know your team is the reason we have so many problems now." Warren's voice had risen almost to a scream.

Daughtrey glared then took a step forward in Warren's face. Teagan planted a hand on his chest to back up.

"Better hold back your pretty boy here." Warren smirked at Daughtrey and tossed a thumb in the air.

Teagan grasped Daughtrey's shoulder and moved in front of him. "It's fine, Daughtrey. Warren's just mad we have kept things under control after his team fucked up the last time."

"We didn't fuck up anything," Warren hissed, nostrils flared.

"Sure about that mission in Virginia?"

He attempted to charge at her, then paused and looked around at the people watching. "Same as your fuck up in Turkey!" Warren barked.

Teagan froze at his comment and Daughtrey looked from Warren to Teagan, not liking her hesitation.

"Aye, we're here to focus on making sure nothing else happens. I suggest you get out of your feelings." Daughtrey faced Teagan and snapped his finger as Warren walked away. "You good, Boss?"

Teagan's eyes flickered open. "I am fine, Daughtrey. People like Warren hate women being in charge. Just ignore him."

Then Daughtrey followed her eyeline of the roped-off area and back to Warren and his team.

"Let me get over here and make sure he doesn't take anything with him."

Teagan waved for her men to start moving in with their supplies. "You got the paperwork. Everything should be left as is for us to go through."

Daughtrey nodded and trekked over to the FBI loading up their SUVs to leave. Teagan walked over to the remnants of the bus and swiped up gloves and foot closures to not leave a trail.

"Make sure to get a picture of everything, Michael. We need to match up everything."

"Sure thing, Teagan."

Teagan propped her hands on her hip. "Casper, I need you to work with Gregory to mock a simulation of the blast."

Casper waved at Gregory and he jogged over to the area.

"Find out if the coroner has anything left of the body," Teagan requested, turned and trekked around the front of the bus seeing the black marks on the ground.

As she roamed around the scene, Teagan casted a hand above her eyes to block out the sun when she noticed a young woman crying near the light pole close to the barrier. Their eyes connected and Emily pulled away, turning her back to move through the blockade when Teagan jogged over to catch up.

"Wait!" Teagan yelled.

Emily speed walked down the street and Daughtrey glanced at Teagan running from the scene, whistling for backup.

Daughtrey waved his hand in the air. "Gregory, back up."

Gregory nodded then took off along with him as more people suddenly watched the commotion. Teagan made it to the alleyway and grasped the fleeing woman by the elbow and held up a hand.

Emily stumbled to the ground crying. "Please."

Teagan bent down to rub her back. "Hey, we're not going to hurt you."

"You don't understand."

Daughtrey, Gregory, and more of her men arrived staring down at them. "Teagan, what's up?"

"What's your name?" Teagan probed.

Emily slowly looked up at Teagan and scrambled to stand. "I have to go."

"Wait! My name is Teagan and we're here to help. Tell me your name."

"Emily."

"Okay, Emily, why were you crying? Did you know anyone on the bus?"

Emily shook her head. "He said-"

Everyone froze at her statement.

"He."

"I have to go, please. He's going to kill me."

Daughtrey blocked her on the left side and Gregory on the right. "Emily."

Teagan raised her hand for them to give her space. "If someone is hurting you, we can protect you."

"The police can't protect me."

Teagan lifted her badge in her right hand, blocking out her team to keep Emily focused on her. "We're not the police."

Her eyes narrowed in confusion. "The Agency," Emily whispered.

Teagan gestured around the circle. "This is Daughtrey, Gregory, and Casper."

"Are you like the Secret Service or something?"

Teagan smiled. "No, much more dangerous."

"We need to get out of here before reporters come asking questions," Daughtrey insisted, noticing people huddled at the end of the street.

"Come with us to just talk."

"You're not arresting me, right? I didn't set this up."

Teagan and Daughtrey's eyes connected at her response. "You won't be arrested," Teagan explained, leading Emily from the alleyway back to the SUV.

Emily climbed in the back and Teagan followed. Next Daughtrey slid into the driver's seat, while Gregory and Casper went back to checking the scene.

"Can you tell me what you meant about set this up?" Teagan probed.

Emily fidgeted with her hands for a moment and wiped the tears from her cheek. "Yesterday, I was walking to the bus stop and got a phone call."

"What school do you go to?"

"Rice University."

As she spoke, Daughtrey looked through the rearview mirror and nodded at Teagan. He was on it. He removed his cell phone and jotted down the information.

"At first I thought it was a prank and I laughed."

"Start from the beginning. Did you recognize the number?"

She shook her head no. "It came up unknown."

"Can you describe the voice? Would you recognize it if you heard it again?"

Emily leaned her head back on the seat. "Yes, it was raspy and creepy -- full of anger."

"Take a deep breath. Close your eyes for me."

"He said I wasn't going to be able to catch the bus because of a car accident."

Daughtrey turned his head to glance at Emily.

"What bus?"

"He knows where I live because a letter came to my door."

"Tell me about the letter."

Emily opened her eyes, peered out of the window and saw a man starring right back at her, the same man that bumped into her on the street.

"Oh my god."

Teagan sat up in her seat and grabbed Emily's hand before she could open the door. "Calm down, Emily. You're safe with us."

Emily raised her hand and pointed. "I saw him before."

Daughtrey jumped out of the car and laid his hand on his holster.

"Hold off, Daughtrey. Emily what do you see?"

Emily swiveled her head back and forth. "The man that bumped into me on the street, that's him. I think he knows something."

"Okay, talk to me. Only way we can help is if you tell the truth."

"They're going to blow up the Capitol building."

Teagan gasped and jumped out of the car. "Get in the car. We have to go now!"

Chapter Four

The barrel of the engine drowned out the noise of oncoming traffic as Daughtrey raced back to the Agency. Teagan held onto Emily's phone and tried to dial the unknown number back to back.

"Still nothing. Has Spider checked in yet?"

Gregory peered at his watch. "Want me to send a car to check on him?"

"Yeah, we need to look at all the files and trace her phone. Get the cameras from the traffic lights," Teagan said, tapping her finger against the dashboard.

The bright sun beamed down as the vehicle swerved up to the gate. Daughtrey extended his hand to verify with security and headed back into the ground floor of the Agency. They parked in their usual spot and each team member piled out of the car. Teagan grasped Emily by the shoulder and ambled to the elevator.

Everyone had stepped on when her phone rang, and she answered as the doors opened and they all headed to the conference room.

"Do you want water, coffee, or something to eat, Emily?"

Daughtrey held the glass door open and Emily took a seat at the end. Gregory sat at the head and logged into the computer.

Emily gazed around the room, then clasped her hands together on top of the table. "Water would be fine."

While Teagan stood and watched Emily closely, her mind replayed each detail Emily talked about and the man that was standing close to the scene of the explosion. Too many variables showed this young woman was too involved somehow, but not the culprit. Right as she was about to take a seat Spider burst in out of breath.

"Just in time."

"Sorry, I had to catch a cab and get out without notice from the group," Spider explained, and pulled out a seat, then motioned to Emily.

"That's Emily. We believe she knows something about the bombing," Daughtrey expressed.

Teagan clasped her hands together as she walked around the room gathering everyone's attention. "Emily, what else happened after bumping into the guy on your way home?"

Emily gulped down more water and lifted her hand to wipe her mouth. "I got home and tried to talk to my roommate, but she thought I was crazy."

Teagan held her hand up in the air. "What's your roommate's name and where is she right now?"

"Rubina Coley. She's at work." Emily stared at Teagan.

"I will get someone to pick her up," Daughtrey said and started typing on his cell.

"So you tell your roommate and then you what, called the police?"

Emily crossed her hands and leaned back in the chair. "After she left for work, I started to call the police, but I got a knock at my door and went to answer, but no one was there."

Teagan, Spider, and Daughtrey's eyes connected.

"Keep going."

Emily exhaled a breath. "I picked up a letter that was left at my door and it read off the address of the U.S. Capitol as the place to be bombed."

Teagan turned to look up at the ceiling, eyes closed in deep thought. It is certain that a major attack on the Capitol would place the U.S. at the heart of the world's terrorist threats, both foreign and domestic, giving them the opportunity to take shots without remorse.

"Do you have the letter on you?" Spider probed.

Emily reached in her pocket and pulled out the envelope and placed it on the table. Spider stood, and grabbed it, reading the information, then passed it to Gregory.

"I can try and see if any handprints remain," Gregory mentioned.

Another bomb going off in a short span of time ran through her mind. Teagan had to come up with some answers before talking to the president.

Teagan rubbed her hands together, then ambled over to the front of the conference room. "Emily, have you shown the letter to anyone outside of your roommate? Think hard because we have to keep this contained."

"No, I actually passed out and when I woke up the next morning and saw the bus, it started to make sense."

"Okay, anything else you remember?"

Emily snapped her finger and sat up straight. "The car accident."

"What car accident?"

"The guy on the phone said I wouldn't get on the bus because of a car accident." Teagan's skin grew hot.

"Gregory."

"Already going through footage at a five-mile radius," Gregory replied, leaned forward, and clicked on the mouse.

While she gazed over the whiteboard, Teagan picked up the eraser and Sharpie and marked up more sections with new information. She knew Emily could be hiding more information, but she needed her to feel comfortable at all times. Teagan gestured to Daughtrey. He stood and marched over to her in the corner.

"Put her up in the family room to talk with the sketch artist. If she wants to go home, keep someone on her." For a moment she pondered over each step in her statements.

"Treating her as a suspect."

"I want to see if they make contact with her again."

"On it, Boss."

Teagan carried on directing the conversation into outlining the timeline on the whiteboard and plugging in more details from Gregory that he noted from watching footage.

Gregory clicked to display the footage on the screen. "Found the car accident." Everyone focused on the projected wall.

Teagan peered at the screen of a woman in a car being hit on the right side by a bus. Gregory enlarged a still photo of the license plate.

"Replay it again."

"She was on the phone," Spider mumbled.

She stepped in closer to watch. "Can you get another angle?"

"I got it as big as it can go," Gregory answered.

Cameras picked up from the opposite side where the bus came in and hit the driver, setting the airbags off and causing the woman to pass out as people ran toward the accident yelling to call the police.

"Her name is Angela Balman, single, no kids," Spider read over her file.

"Is she still alive?"

Spider handed the copy to them. "Yeah, still at the hospital. Probably could get over there and get an update."

Teagan tapped her finger against her thigh. "Any police reports?"

"Clean. We can try and get a conversation with the bus driver as well." Gregory studied each frame and loaded up his flash drive.

"Spider, you go with Gregory to talk to the bus driver. I will talk to Angela."

He swiped up the rest of the files. "Are you sure?"

"Yes, it might be better showing up alone."

Spider stood as Gregory shut down his computer and hopped up to leave. Her team was capable of many things, especially when being backed into a corner. Finding the culprits might lead to a bigger issue, but Teagan knew leaving the door open to have more incidents wouldn't be good for the next director that steps into the role.

* * *

Immediately when the truck stopped Spider, Gregory, and Casper hopped out of the car. They rushed through the hospital doors and stepped to the receptionist's window. Spider cupped his badge in hand and smiled as the young lady grinned back. "I need the room number to Angela Balman."

"Are you family?" she investigated.

"No, we are working on a time sensitive case, if you hadn't seen about the explosion."

"Does she have something to do with that? Oh my god!" The older, grey haired nurse pushed her glasses above her head and reached to pick up the phone.

Spider snatched the receiver out of her hand. "Ma'am, I need you to calm down. Nothing is going on right now. We just need her room number."

"I knew she looked suspicious. She's probably working with the guy that came here yesterday asking about her."

"What guy?" Gregory probed.

She shrugged. "Some man that had a low-cut spiky haircut. Tall, thinly built asked about her and said she was his sister."

Spider and Gregory glanced at each other.

"We need her room number." Gregory cut his eyes toward her.

"Well, she's in room twenty-two. Is something wrong?"

Spider, Gregory, and Casper sprinted down the hall as security, a young nurse, and few people in the emergency room looked on.

Instead of waiting for the elevator, the team jogged to the emergency exit and up the stairs, then Gregory yanked the door open to a quiet reception area.

"Stay out here and watch for anything and see if you can get the nurse to get access to the video of when Angela received visitors," Spider directed, motioning toward the room.

Gregory darted to the nurses' station as Spider gently knocked on the door and pushed it open to a dark room with only the TV monitor playing. Spider squinted his eyes, drawn to the bed with Angela curled up under the covers. He approached and motioned for Casper to check the bathroom.

"Angela," Spider whispered.

Casper came out of the bathroom shaking his head.

"Angela Balman," Spider called out and lifted the covers back off her head and dropped his back in frustration at seeing Angela eye's wide open, hands laid alongside her. He placed fingers on the side of her neck to check for pulse.

"No signs of life."

Casper scanned the room for any evidence. "How do you want to handle this now?"

"I need to see the doctor that worked on her and talk with any relatives."

Casper pushed his long fingers through his hair. "Teagan's going to be pissed."

Spider reached into his pocket and dragged his phone out to make a call. "I don't blame her."

Gregory marched in the room and frowned as he arrived close to the bedside.

Teagan answered, wind in the background. "Tell me some good news."

At his back he paced back and forth, as the doctor and nurse arrived. "Not looking good."

"Is she not talking?" Teagan checked.

"She's dead," Spider replied.

"Fuck! How is that possible?" Teagan demanded. Her voice had a savage edge to it.

"The doctor just came so let me get some information and we can meet back up."

"Alright, keep me posted." Teagan disconnected the call.

"What happened here? Are you the police?" Doctor Matt Shrouder commanded, then stuck his hand out to Spider.

"Something like that. We're working on the car crash and wanted to speak with Angela."

"Angela was alive the last time I checked her over, so I am not understanding how she's dead and you're in her room," Doctor Shrouder pondered.

"Doctor Shrouder, we are asking the questions here. When is the last time you saw her alive and talking?"

"We need the camera footage of the time she arrived," Gregory explained.

"I can't authorize that."

"Sir, at this moment, we are in a national emergency so the authorization is not needed when it comes to the public's safety, and I can promise my boss hates hearing the word no."

"Are you the FBI or Homeland Security? I mean, do I need to get a lawyer?"

Spider cut the distance and slipped his hands in pockets. "That's up to you."

Doctor Shrouder raked a hand down his neck. He turned to pick up the chart hanging on the wall. "I saw her yesterday around six pm before I left for the day, and the charge nurses never came in for follow-up." He frowned at the discovery.

"So anyone could have come in here and did something to her. Is what you're saying basically?"

"You have to understand we've been short-staffed for weeks," he pleaded.

"What were her symptoms when she was brought here?"

"Broken hip, lung collapsed, a head injury. She could have been on a full recovery in time with the right support."

"I need a report on her cause of death."

Doctor Shrouder ambled to the left side of the bed and checked over Angela for any signs of bruises.

"That will take a few days."

Spider stomped out of the room, and narrowed his eyes on the nurses' station, then his gaze aimed up to the cameras in the corners. "You have five hours." He turned back to the doctor.

The doctor nodded his head at the security guard approaching.

"Is everything good, Doctor Shrouder?"

"These men say they're from some government agency, but I have a dead patient and they were caught in her room."

Before the guard could speak, Spider pushed his hand toward his badge hanging around his neck.

"Doctor Shrouder is under the impression he's running things. We will have the entire wing shut down until we get what we want, and Doctor you will be under arrest," Spider informed him.

"Wait! Wait! Okay, let me go look," Doctor Shrouder stated.

The security guard shrugged, walked back to his station and stared at the video monitors.

Chapter Five

Teagan stared at the white picket fence and the large brick home of Angela Balman that held a rose garden stacked in front of the step's corner. The temperature being a cool eighty, the weatherman mentioned a cloudy night bringing rain to the area. Teagan stepped forward and glanced around the neighborhood as her driver stood outside of the truck. Once Spider explained Angela's death, it all started turning in her mind. Another explosion was stirring soon and time was ticking. As she raised her hand to knock, the door flew open.

"Hello, can I help you?" the older woman with shoulder length hair and a wide smile greeted. Teagan could tell by her eyes she was related to Angela. They both had greenish-blue irises and dimples in both cheeks.

"Hi, I understand Angela is in the hospital."

"Oh, have you spoken with her?"

Teagan cleared her throat and looked back over her shoulder.

"Can we speak inside?"

The woman dropped the smile. "Is something wrong? The bus was at fault."

"Are you related to Angela?"

She held the dish towel to her chest. "Yes, she's my daughter. I came to visit like I do every year and when they called and told me she was in an accident I drove up to the hospital."

"What's your name?"

"Mariel."

Teagan extended her hand out for Mariel and pointed at the couch to see if it was okay to take a seat.

"Yes, please have a seat. Would you like some water, tea, or coffee?"

"No, ma'am. I am so sorry to tell you, but Angela didn't make it."

Mariel jumped up from the couch with her hand to her heart. "What! I just talked to the doctor and Angela yesterday."

"What did she talk with you about?" Teagan hated to use the opportunity to get more details on the car crash, but more people could be in trouble.

Mariel rubbed her forehead as she paced the floor. "Mostly she was happy to be getting better and we talked about her needing more surgeries down the road."

"So you talked to her directly?"

There were times like this Teagan hated to be in her role, and all she could give people weren't lies, but slanted truths.

"How did she die? I mean, are you sure it was Angela Balman?"

"Is there someone I could call for you?"

Mariel shook her head. "It was just me and Angela

after her father died two years ago. I live in Seattle, so we only saw each other about once or twice a year."

Teagan rose from the couch and moved to the fireplace. She lifted the picture frame of Angela as a little girl with her parents.

"Does Angela have any boyfriends?"

"No, she's been single for a while. Work was her life."

"Any friends you know that could come here to be with you?"

"Why do I feel like my questions are being ignored? Tell me the truth about my daughter."

Teagan turned to Mariel and strolled back to the couch with the picture in her hand. "Angela was murdered."

Mariel's head jerked back, her mouth dropped open. "Murdered?"

"Can you tell me anything about the last few days you spent with her?" Teagan asked, placing the picture frame on the table.

"Any phone calls or weird behavior?"

Mariel burst into tears and shook her head. "All we did was go out to eat a few nights, to the farmers market, and watched movies. My God, who would want to hurt my baby?" Mariel replied, jumped up and swiped a tissue from the box.

Teagan knew Mariel was in pain, and finding out your child was killed because of a potential terrorist act would be a major blow. Right now her concern was getting the person or persons responsible before something else happened.

"Okay, I will need a list of her friends, job, and family members she's stayed in contact with over the last few years."

"You still haven't answered my question."

"Mariel-"

She held up her hand, interrupting Teagan. "I can handle the truth, please."

"Did you hear about the explosion?" Teagan asked and stared at Mariel's mannerisms, to find any hesitations or questionable behavior.

"Yes, but what does that have to do with my daughter?"

"Nothing so far. I am piecing things together and need your help."

"Do you have children?"

"I do."

"If this happened to one of them what would you do?"

She sighed and clasped her hands together. "I would want answers and the people brought to justice."

"That's all I ask of you. I will get the lists for you. Let me grab my phone book." Mariel ambled off down the hall.

Teagan's gaze fell around the living room. Bright colorful curtains hung high. Plants inside matched the gardens outside. Teagan scanned the coffee table with the answering machine and mail lingering. She sauntered by and gently pushed them aside one by one to see all having to deal with bill payments.

Mariel walked back in and held up a sheet of paper. "Here you go. I hope it helps."

Teagan smiled. "Have you checked the messages yet? I see it beeping."

Mariel looked down at the end table. "Actually I forgot all about it after I woke up today." She pressed the play button.

"Hey Mariel, call me back. I was going to take Angela some soup like I promised," the message stated.

"Who's the woman on the voicemail?"

Mariel grinned and reached to pick up the landline phone. "Constance, her best friend."

Teagan grabbed her wrist to stop her. "When's the last time Constance saw Angela?"

"Uh, I guess two days ago. I was in and out of the hospital because I needed rest."

"So Constance was visiting her every day?"

"Yeah, they're best friends. Why do you ask?"

Teagan strolled to the door. "No reason. I will have my team reach out to you about Angela's remains."

"Thank you, Teagan, and please find the person that hurt my baby."

More clues of unraveling helped propel Teagan's search into a bigger path of secrets she hoped wouldn't lead to more deaths. The door shut behind her as she jogged down the stairs back to the awaiting truck when a few kids on bikes rode up and down the street. She watched as they played together with no cares in the world. To them it was how life was supposed to be -- free, whimsical, and fun. In the Agency's mind, the work they did enabled those thoughts of nothing was bad in the world because of the amount of people that were caught and put away for trying to destroy their country.

"Where are we off to now?"

"Home, I need to clear my head and being with my family does that."

"Home it is."

* * *

Laughter and a loud TV blasted through the walls as Teagan unlocked the door with a smile on her face. She tossed her keys in the glass bowl and kicked off her shoes and jacket. All three of her kids sat in the living room watching a movie at the highest volume.

"Hi, Mom!" all three kids screamed at the same time.

Teagan walked behind the couch and kissed each one on top of their heads.

Teagan pushed two fingers in her ear to drown out the noise. "Why is it so loud?"

"We wanted the full experience!" CJ yelled.

Her oldest son was more and more handsome every time she saw him. While being in sports he'd become a star in soccer and basketball. While still getting good grades, his coaches filled her and Christian in on how CJ was a leader and how all of the kids looked up to him. Teagan reached for the remote and turned the volume down.

"Boo, Mommy." Tatum frowned, then turned it into a cheeky smile.

Teagan chuckled. "It was too loud. Have you all eaten yet?"

"Dad said we can have pizza tonight," CJ recalled.

"Pizza."

"Yep, we've been good and not bothered him while he works." Tatum grinned.

Teagan laughed and headed to the back of the house and knocked on Chrisitan's office door. "Hey, babe."

Christian turned in his chair and pulled his glasses down. "When did you get home?"

Teagan sauntered farther in and reached her arms out for a hug. "Just now."

He rubbed a hand up and down her back. "You look tired."

"I'm exhausted, but need to still talk with the guys."

"Are things looking good or will we need to go back to the office?"

"Honestly, I'm not sure. I feel in my gut another bomb is going to go off, and if so it's the U.S. Capitol."

"The U.S. Capitol!" he barked, fists balled hard in rage.

Teagan raised her hands to cover his mouth. "Christian, I don't want to scare the kids."

He started to pace in front of his desk. "Sorry. I mean, the U.S. Capitol. Teagan, what is going on for real?"

Teagan turned her back to lean against it. "Still trying to figure it out."

Chrisitan opened his mouth to speak when the doorbell rang. "Dad, I need the money for the pizza." CJ barged in his office with his hand out.

Christian stood and slipped a hand into his pocket, removed his wallet and counted out fifty dollars.

"Leave a tip."

"Okay!" CJ shouted and ran back to pay.

"Come on. Let's go monitor the pizza brigade before it all falls apart."

Teagan froze at his statement. "What did you say?"

"I said, come on so we can monitor the boys with the pizza."

Teagan gripped him by the arm. "Before it all falls apart."

"Yeah."

"It was all being monitored and the plan is make sure nothing falls apart."

"Honey, it's just pizza."

Teagan waved her hands in the air. "No, Christian you're a genius."

"Yes, I am a genius."

Teagan pecked him on the lips and walked with him out of the room. "From the moment Angela was hit by the bus, which is monitored on cameras and traffic lights. Plus, the call to Emily, everything is linked together somehow and with Angela dying they want to make sure nothing falls apart."

"Emily, who's that?"

"Someone I need to make sure has protection twenty-four seven."

"Where are you going?"

Teagan ran back in his office and grabbed her cell from her purse. "To make a call. Make sure the kids wash up before they eat."

Mariel's accounts of seeing Angela and the time of her death should have the tracking of the last people to see her and the person that dropped off the note to Emily.

"Hey, Boss, at the bar grabbing food," Daughtrey said when the call connected.

"Add extra protection around Emily, I think she might be next."

"Okay, did something new come in we need to know about?"

"Is Spider with you?"

"Yeah, we should be back at the office soon to run everything together."

"Alright, first thing in the morning we need a full download. I have some thoughts, but we have to keep Emily alive."

"Are you worried someone is after her for a reason?"

"I will tell you in the morning. Just be careful, Daughtrey."

"Always, Boss."

Teagan hung up, bit her bottom lip, closed her eyes then scanned Christian's office before walking back to the kitchen and taking a seat.

Tatum hovered over the table. "Mom, CJ is eating all of the pizza," she complained then she stuck her lip out in a pout and groaned.

"CJ, be nice and share."

CJ lifted his right arm and bent it to show his small muscles. "I'm a growing boy. The ladies love me so I have to eat more."

Teagan rolled her eyes. "Who told you that?"

"My girlfriend."

Teagan and Christian locked eyes before looking at CJ.

"Girlfriend? CJ, you're too young for a girlfriend."

"Dad said he had a girlfriend at my age." CJ pointed at his father.

Teagan glared and picked up a napkin.

Christian rubbed his temple and exhaled a breath. "CJ, eat your food, please."

"Ohh, he has cooties!" Tatum jested.

"Shut up!" CJ shouted back and stuck out his tongue.

Teagan clapped her hands together to calm them down, then pointed at Tatum to sit in the chair correctly. "Hey, you two, be nice and share."

"Mom, are we going back to your job? It was fun eating all the candy," Cole said.

"Not sure, but you need to stop eating so much candy before you get cavities."

"It was fun playing games and Daughtrey owes me money."

Teagan smirked and gulped her water. "Daughtrey?"

"Yep. We bet on Basketball Two-K. If I won, he has to pay me twenty dollars."

Teagan and Christian laughed at his comment. She extended a hand to rub his palm. "Well, I will let him know to pay up."

Chapter Six

The wind brushed against his skin as he marched down the street and stood in front of the barrier sign that stated no admittance, and scanned his surrounding area. Perry held up his phone and snapped a few pictures, then recorded video of people entering and leaving the visitors' section. It looked much more prominent on TV, but in person, it was like a small mansion a kid would play with for fun. The traffic moved in and out at slow speeds. A few people on the sidewalk lined up for visitor entry. So far their plan was coming together without any interruptions, while the other side of the city was up in arms over the bus explosion. He took another minute to take in the tourists then started to walk back to the van, then climbed inside. Perry scrolled to the photo album, clicked out to his email and forwarded the pictures and video to his other contact.

"Did they give you any problems?" Samson probed.

He shook his head and smiled. "No, I looked just like any other tourist."

"Good, what are we going to do about Emily?"

"She's still being watched. Might need to send someone who can get through security to take her out."

Samson's mouth was set in a grim line, his jaw tense. "He won't like that we're coming back to him."

Perry's eyes darted back and forth from traffic to Samson. "Doesn't matter. He's in it now too deep."

As they spoke and weaved into traffic, his phone rang. "Speaking of him."

Samson gestured with a snap of his fingers. "Put it on speaker."

Perry placed the phone in the cup holder, locking on his seatbelt. "We were just talking about you."

"I can imagine," their contact surmised.

Samson laced his fingers together in his lap, an uneasy feeling in his stomach. "We need Emily taken out."

"So take her out."

"She has protection around her. You have it easier to go around those checkpoints," Perry pointed out.

They'd spent years and months planning to take out one of the most significant of America's cherished land-marks. It not only symbolized the USA, but the benefit of the plan was to tarnish and taint the political structure that was willed by the president. On top of Teagan Stone losing everything and being seen as a coward when she lacked the courage to the American people and the Agency. He could hear the hesitation in his voice, but the plan was already in motion.

"Everything is lined up to happen within two days. Before it can happen, we need Emily to die." Samson's bushy brows squeezed together, and he jabbed his index finger on the top of the dashboard.

"Didn't you already take care of Angela? It should be easier for you to do Emily."

They pulled up to the side of the street near their apartment where they held protests, and eased down the alleyway, trekked to the back door of the building. Both men shook hands with Megan, who they brought in later to work with them. She'd always felt like regular people were being ignored and the only way to break up the system was to make noise. Spread out on the table were blueprints of the White House she'd picked up along with her morning cup of coffee, and handed him a new phone from her hand.

"Make sure everything is wiped from it before you destroy it," Perry reminded her, and gulped down the coffee.

Megan removed the SIM card and read over text threads. "How did everything go when you made it to the front entrance of the White House?" she asked.

"No one suspected a thing. I was just another person wanting to take pictures and video. I got a lot of good shots," Perry said, rubbing his nose.

They studied her face for a long moment.

"Are we sure we can make it happen?"

Perry shrugged, tossed the cup in the trash and picked up the breakfast sandwich and took a bite.

"We have no choice. We've come this far."

"I think we need to run over everything one more time," Megan suggested, face crinkled in concern.

"Megan is right. We have only one chance to get it right," Samson agreed.

Perry leaned against the counter with his arms crossed and stroked his beard. "Alright, I have to be at the location between six and eight am and plant the bombs in both ends of the White House."

"While you're doing that Samson and I will hold a

protest at the same time." Megan disengaged the phone and cracked it down into pieces.

Samson, Megan, and Perry all hated what the government had done with the false lies and bleeding of their families. Their contact reached out about taking matters into their own hands not only to get revenge for Jeffrey's death, but they'd come up with a lot of money that nobody would ever refuse.

"We only have thirty minutes to get it set up, so you have to stay focused -- no hiccups," Perry mentioned, then sipped more of the coffee.

"Then we meet back here and set it off while everyone else thinks the Capitol is going to be destroyed, when it's really the White House." Megan smiled, and gleefully rubbed her hands together.

Samson picked up the black Sharpies and marked the checkpoint of each step on the blueprint. "Are we sure your contact won't fuck us over?" Samson asked, then chewed on his breakfast wrap.

"He's deeper in this shit than we are. If he tries anything I have proof that will bring him down."

"Good. Emily's already gone to the authorities. Are we going to get rid of her like Angela?" Megan wondered. She stood to drop the phone scraps in the trash.

"I called to set it up for her to be taken out beforehand so nothing traces back to us."

Megan leaned her elbow on top of the counter. "He give you any pushback?"

"Hesitant at first, but I reiterated how this is something that could backfire on us and we will gladly take him down with us." Perry's face became dark and impassive.

"Then we're all set to complete our part and they'll be none the wiser when we are out of the country."

Samson removed a cigarette and lighter from his pocket. "The boat pickup to Cuba is already planned. Then we can fly out to our next checkpoint in London."

Perry stared down at the blueprints in awe as a grin formed on his face. Megan snapped her fingers in his face.

"Hey, what about Angela's death? Anybody snooping around? I made sure to keep things clear for Samson when he came up there."

"Her doctor got paid off. He won't do any talking unless he wants to go down with us," Samson explained.

"Still. We need to keep a close eye on him."

"You never threw away your nurse's uniform, correct?"

Megan brushed a hand down her arms. "No, I have it in the closet."

"Then keep it for now and if anyone comes back up there we can have you steer them in a different direction. Her mother talked to that Teagan woman the other day."

A vibration on his phone interrupted their conversation and he slipped it out to read the message.

Unknown: T.S. at Angela's home.
Perry: How do you know?
Unknown: Staring at the car.

Perry jolted up from the chair and paced back and forth.

Samson walked back into the kitchen. "What happened?"

"Teagan's at Angela's place," Perry informed her and sent a message back.

Unknown: Keep me updated.

Perry stared at the pictures of Teagan going in and out of the house within an hour. He passed the phone to Samson, then Megan.

"Maybe you should go back to the hospital for the next few days as a precaution," Samson said, raised up from the chair and picked up the bag off the floor. He unzipped it, revealing a few loads of explosives and guns.

"I met someone from the rally. Maybe he could be useful."

"What do you mean?" Perry asked.

Megan slipped her hand in her back pocket and removed her cell and held it up for the men to see.

"I got his number and he seemed to be down for the cause."

Perry gazed down at the phone number and name. "Terrance."

"He walked up on us while we protested and asked how he could be helpful for the team with getting our truth out."

Perry frowned. He grasped her elbow. "That sounds weird... a random guy noticed you and wanted to join. Did you say anything about us?"

Megan reared her head back and snatched her arm out of his grip. "No, he seemed fine. I could pick out a cop a mile away and besides, we already have people in our back pocket that no one would suspect."

"We already have the three of us and the people that feel like we're really protesting for a cause. It would be too many people to keep on track."

"I just think it's one more person who we use to do

our bidding and leave with the police talking to better than the three of us." Megan winked her left eye.

"No, the way we can control things is by limiting our hands in every bucket."

"Sounds like you want to try and control things when we're a team that makes decisions together," Megan pouted then sighed.

"No need to fight. Perry is right. That guy would need to be vetted and we're out of time."

"All I am saying is that we could easily push him to the forefront as the scapegoat while we get away to Cuba."

Samson separated packs of money from the bag and split it three ways. "We decided to keep it just the three of us. Now what's more important is making sure Emily is silenced. On top of that, we have your badge and ID for the gardening job you've been hired to do on the lawn." Samson reached in the bag and pulled out the fake ID for Perry and handed it to him.

"Completely clean right?"

"Nothing can be traced back to you or any of us. The social matched to a dead person that I changed out and it won't come back for a while. And besides they're going to be too jammed up with the chaos of the bomb to even think about us."

Perry trekked out of the kitchen down the hall to the living room, plopped down on the couch and picked up the remote from the table then turned to the news.

Megan came in behind him and stood behind the couch with the latest reports of the bus tragedy running.

"The family of the bus driver has set the funeral for the upcoming weekend and expressed thanks to everyone that has reached out with prayers and flowers," the DCKY news anchor informed.

Megan nudged him on the shoulder. "Turn it up."

Samson came from the back carrying the bag and placed it inside the closet near the front door. "It might be time for us to get out of this apartment. We've been here for a week. We can't stay put too long... might get people thinking."

"Megan, secure another place for us tonight, something on the far end of the city that people couldn't trace."

"Sure thing. I am heading to go take a nap," Megan responded, and jogged up the stairs.

Samson slapped Perry on the arm and pointed toward the stairs. "You and Megan having problems?"

Perry stared up in the direction she went. "She's getting too in her head. We might need to let her go."

Samson blew out a breath. "Already?"

"She's taking things too far and needs to understand the purpose and goal."

"Well, it might help keep the money not be split three ways."

Perry smirked. "Exactly. That's all I care about."

"Soon as we get the job done, we can take her out."

"That's what I am thinking, she'd be one less problem the police will have to connect to you and me."

Samson's stomach growled. "I'm going to grab some food before we go back out to scope out the area."

"Make enough for me."

Samson waved his hand in the air and walked off.

* * *

Hours later Megan yawned in the back of the van and sipped the hot cup of tea. This was their fifth night watching the people work at the White House late at night. While Samson took his nap, Megan wrote down each shift time and the number of people that came in and out from each door.

"Look there. You see the security patrolling together."

"We have to use silencers to keep the noise down."

"I agree. The moment we show our hands we're back at square one and thrown in jail."

"True. I will only have a certain amount of time to get it set."

Samson snored loudly and Megan frowned at the disturbance. "We have four people that are coming to protest with us while you're putting the explosives out."

"As long as you time it right to get an audience, we should be fine."

Megan leaned her head on his shoulder. "I am glad we get to do this together."

Perry smiled and pressed a kiss on her forehead. "I told you when I came up with the idea we would be rich."

"I know, but the amount of time we've spent going over every inch and how we could get caught had me worried."

"Nothing to worry about, as long as you stick to the plan."

While they watched, another vehicle passed by and pulled up to the gate. Megan stared at the time on the clock and saw it was going on midnight. Two men stepped out and a woman shaking hands with the staff. Megan removed the binoculars and nudged Perry on the shoulder.

"Look at that."

Perry took the binoculars from her hand to see the people walking away. "Probably more staff."

"They didn't look dressed like the normal staff."

"Are you sure?"

"Yeah. Maybe we should check with your contact."

"Too late to call him and right now he should be handling our other problems."

"I have a weird feeling, Perry."

"You worry too much."

"Staff usually aren't driving up in a blacked-out SUV."

Perry glanced again in the direction of where Megan was talking and squinted his eyes. "We can wait them out and try to get a license plate."

Megan rolled her eyes, turned and nudged him on the leg. "Samson, wake up."

Samson groggily rubbed his eyes and sat forward. "What?"

"Check out the black SUV up ahead."

"I think it's nothing, but Megan is saying it could be someone outside of staff," Perry informed Samson, then passed the binoculars over to him.

Samson held them up to his eyes and watched people talk back and forth as the car sat in the front. "Just a car."

"To you, but I have a feeling we should follow them when they leave."

"We have no time for car chases, Megan," Samson groaned.

"Perry, have I been wrong about anything else so far?"

Perry looked from Megan to Samson, then back at the side entrance. "If they come out in the next few minutes we can follow."

"Since when are we taking orders from Megan?" Samson grunted.

"I am a part of the team, and I have a hunch we should check all precautions."

"She's right."

"Fine, do what your girlfriend says," Samson muttered.

"Fuck you, Samson." Megan flipped him off and tossed her cup out the window. Moments later the three people emerged and hopped back in the vehicle. The SUV pulled around the drive and waited for the gates to open and drove in the opposite direction of Perry's van. Megan raised her hand and gestured. "Follow them before you lose it in traffic."

Perry turned the key in the ignition, flicked the light switch and moved in behind the car a few feet away. "Relax, we have plenty of time. Grab a pen and paper to get their license plate."

"The only people that stop by the White House late at night have a job to do for the president that can't be explained to the public," Samson muttered.

"We will know for sure soon. Look. They're turning off at the light," Megan commented. She sat forward to jot the number down.

"It's blacked out except for the last two letters AG," Perry stated.

Megan and Perry turned to face each other.

"What does AG stand for in DC?"

"FBI or DEA possibly?"

"No that would be too obvious."

"Doesn't matter. They're getting on the freeway. Stay away a good distance," Samson announced.

Perry raked a hand down his face. "I think they made

us. He's moving in and out of lanes," Perry hissed, slamming his hand on the steering wheel.

"We have to stick to the plan or everything we've worked for is gone."

Megan motioned at the upcoming off-ramp. "Samson is right. If we run now, they will know something is up. Turn at the next exit like any of the other cars."

"Did you get the new place picked out? We can't go back to the old apartment to sleep."

"All of our shit is there."

"Drive around for a little bit to see if they catch on. If they don't, we can head to the apartment for the night."

"She's right. Play it off. At this time of night, people are out eating."

"AG," Megan mumbled under her breath.

Perry sat back in thought and looked out of the rearview mirror as he pulled up to a light near a restaurant. "Stop in here and wait it out."

All three piled out of the car and sat to eat in the local cafe that only held a few people inside since it was after midnight.

Chapter Seven

Daughtrey's eyes dragged back to the road and captured the last minutes of Teagan's statement as he pulled up to the gate of the Agency. "Something has you distracted."

Daughtrey raked a hand up to his beard. "It's probably nothing, but I could have sworn we were being followed when we left the White House."

Teagan squinted her eyes at him. "Are you sure?"

He nodded. "Maybe sleep will help, but my gut says a car was staying a few feet away, but jumped when I moved into another lane."

Spider climbed out of the vehicle and stretched his arms. "Who would be following us this late? Not like we have to give our locations out to anyone." Spider leaned against the truck, arms folded.

Teagan reached in her pocket and removed her phone. "How long do you feel we had a tail?"

Daughtrey lifted his bulletproof vest off. "Maybe five minutes. It was so fast."

A summons by the president to come and discuss

updates on the explosion had Teagan and the team leaving from investigating Emily's place. "Hey, Albert. Can you get the camera footage for about a three-block radius of the White House?" Teagan spoke into her phone and stood in front of them.

Teagan hit the red button and tucked it back in her pocket. "He will have the video sent over in the morning. Go home and get some rest. We can't do anything at the moment."

"We probably spooked them," Spider deduced.

Daughtrey stuck his hand out to Spider and reached for Teagan in a tight hug.

Spider chucked his chin up in the air. "See y'all tomorrow." Spider slapped hands with a few other agents in the garage.

Jason waited at the vehicle for her as she eased in the passenger seat. Teagan slouched down and closed her eyes.

"Back home?"

"Yep. Need to get some hours of sleep before we go back to the president with answers."

He backed out of a parking space and drove up to the gate, turned left. "I have confidence you will catch the person responsible."

"Thanks, but as you know if we find one, more start to pop up and the cycle continues."

"That's why we have you, Boss Lady. Never doubt yourself."

Teagan smiled as they cruised down the road headed back to her home. Within ten minutes, they arrived and said goodbye. She set the alarm, trekked through the house, checked in on each of her kids for the night and said a silent prayer. Teagan tossed her badge and keys on the nightstand, bent on the edge of the bed and removed her shoes. Deciding to shower in the morning, she changed into large T-shirt, slipped into bed and fell asleep as Christian wrapped a hand around her waist.

* * *

CJ rushed into the kitchen behind his little sister holding up her doll, as Teagan poured orange juice for everyone, with the TV blaring in the background. Mornings with her whole family gave her peace and she loved the moments when she could just be a mom and wife. Christian fixed each plate of pancakes, eggs, and sausage, handed them off to everyone, then took a seat. Teagan sat opposite him and grasped his hand, then said a silent prayer.

"Leave your sister alone, CJ."

"Dad, you don't understand. She's coming in my room."

Tatum picked up the fork and knife and cut into her food. "No, I don't." Then stuck her tongue out at him.

The table erupted in laughter.

"What are the plans for today? You don't have practice after school," Teagan probed.

"Can we go to the movies?"

"Yes! I want to see the new Disney movie!" Tatum exclaimed.

Christian and Teagan made eye contact briefly.

"Well, if you behave for your teacher, your father will take you."

"Why can't you come?"

"Remember I told you we have a big case I'm working on for my boss."

"Oh right," Tatum replied, as she licked the syrup off her finger.

Cole hopped up to grab his baseball bookbag. "Mom, can you take us to school?"

Teagan clasped a hand around the cup of coffee. "Why are you in a rush?"

"He's trying out for the baseball team to impress a girl," Tatum taunted, puckering her lips to pretend kissing.

Everyone laughed and Cole pushed her shoulder, and she giggled. Christian and CJ stood up and grabbed their plates to take to the sink.

"Be nice. Cole, yes. I will be taking you three to school."

Seconds later, the kids came out of the house and ran to jump in the car; Teagan hugged her husband.

"Tatum, stop hitting your brother."

Ring!

Teagan reached in her pocket and pulled her phone out to see an unknown number. "Teagan here."

"I sent the footage to you from last night, not much to see."

Teagan rolled up her sleeve and looked at her watch. "Were you able to get a license plate number?"

Albert is Head of Security at the White House and a former member of the Agency. "Partial number, sending to your phone now."

"Thanks, Albert. I should be at the office soon to check it out."

"He wanted to get a debrief on why you needed the footage pulled."

Teagan sighed as they appeared at the school. "Let me call you back. I have my kids with me."

"Should we be alarmed?" Albert asked.

Teagan watched CJ and Cole jump out of the car. "Give me some time to confirm. Talk soon." Teagan hung up and smiled toward her kids.

Tatum reached for her hand as the boys ran off to head into the building.

Teagan ran a hand down Tatum's back and bent down for a hug. "Be good today, babygirl. Love you."

"Love you too, Mommy." Tatum stretched her arms around Tatum's neck.

Finally back in the car Teagan bit her bottom lip, scrolled through her email and clicked on the file sent by Albert.

Traffic was clear on the main roads headed back to the office. Teagan rewatched the video over and over of the same black van that looked like it was from the early nineties parked two blocks from the White House.

She enhanced her phone screen over the still picture of the driver, unable to get a clear shot.

"He looks familiar."

Soon as the car approached the reserved space for her vehicle she reached for her bag, purse, and keys and waved bye. She stepped out to speak to the rest of the guards on duty. Teagan stepped on the elevator, held up her ID for the doors to close and pressed the top floor. Seconds later the ding came and she walked through the hall, smiling at a few staff members. After Teagan unlocked her office door, she tossed her things on top of her desk and pulled up her email on her computer.

Knock, Knock!

Teagan removed her jacket and slipped on glasses and leaned forward at the screen. "Come in."

Celine grinned holding her usual mug in her hand. "Boss, here's your coffee and messages."

"Thank you."

"The guys are here ready to debrief in the conference room," Celine expressed.

Teagan stretched her hand to take the list of messages and read through everything, then replayed the video again.

"Anything new with the bus situation?"

"No, not yet."

"My mom still rides the bus and this has her nervous."

"If you want, we can get her a driver until we have it under control. I know she works far away."

Celine smiled. "Thanks, Boss, but I never want special treatment."

Teagan scoffed. "That is not special treatment. You and your family are important to us here."

"Thanks for always looking out for me and my family."

"I told you to call me Teagan."

She chuckled and watched Teagan stand up and grab her coffee. "Let me get back to the front."

"Hold my calls unless it's Christian or my kids. I think we're going out so will need silence."

"You need backup called."

Teagan blew out a breath, and they walked down the hall to the conference room. "Do me a favor and get an update on Emily's security."

Her brows drew together. "She's the one that came here the other day."

"I have a feeling she might be in danger."

"On it, Teagan."

Teagan rubbed her shoulder. "Thank you." Teagan

turned and pushed open the conference room door and glanced at the front center with all the information they'd gathered on the case. Everyone said good morning and Teagan gulped the rest of her coffee down. She exhaled and raked a hand through her braids.

"How are we looking? I have some things to run down."

Daughtrey turned to face the whiteboard and stood up. "What we do know is that Angela was hit by a bus, while talking on the phone. At the same time, Emily was preparing to get on a bus with them both getting phone calls."

"Timeline is minutes within each other. Syncing up means they're connected since the routes match up," Spider explained.

Gregory typed on the computer. "Angela died in the hospital and we know someone killed her because she died being smothered and the nurse that worked that night is missing."

Teagan tapped her finger to her chin. "You think the nurse is connected somehow."

"We listened to the doctor, but shit sounded weird."

Broderick stuck his head inside and shut it behind him.

"Surprised to see you here, man."

Broderick slapped hands with Daughtrey and Spider and stared at Teagan. "I finished another case I was leading and thought I would come and help you guys out."

"We can use all the help we can get," Spider responded. He cocked his head at Teagan.

Broderick stood with his hands in his pockets. "If Teagan says it's cool."

"Sit. We can use all the help we can get. Spider continue."

"I could be wrong, but when I looked at the picture of the nurse from the video, she matched the girl at the protest."

Teagan glared at him. "Say that one more time."

"When we got a clear picture and talked with the doctor, I was able to pinpoint her as being the woman at the protest."

"They're all working together."

"Have to be." Daughtrey picked up the marker at the dry erase board and jotted down notes.

"What's the connection?"

"Put your eyes on someone or something else while they plan out a bigger event," Broderick muttered, lifting the picture off the table.

"Albert sent over the footage from last night. Gregory, pull it up for me and compare it to the hospital photo. For the guy and girl."

Gregory jumped into gear and typed on his computer. "Give me a second."

Teagan rose up and walked up to the front of the room near Daughtrey and Spider. She pointed her finger at the screen of the photos. "We have one woman dead, a bomb on a bus, and Emily under protection. No witnesses would be their next move, right?"

"If I were them, I would make sure to take her out before I set off another one," Broderick suggested.

"I agree."

Celine appeared with a distraught look on her face. "Teagan, can I talk to you?"

Teagan motioned for her to come in and speak. "Is something wrong with my family?"

"No, they're fine. It's the security detail on Emily. They're not answering."

"How many people did you request?" Spider asked.

Teagan crossed her hands over her chest. "At least ten, plus the building should have security separate from our people."

"We should get there," Broderick said.

"Broderick's right. I feel like something is going down in the next day or two. Albert found one car that pulled up a few feet away from us last night."

Daughtrey snapped his fingers. "I was right."

Gregory shook his head and threw his hands on top of his head. "Yep, and it's the same people from the hospital."

The facial recognition matched a hundred percent on the screen between both photos of the man and woman.

"I bet that's the guy Emily saw if we can get her to ID him," Daughtrey mentioned.

"We can't bring her up here. We have to be cautious if they're following us still or her. It might spook them to set the bomb off sooner."

The entire team trailed Teagan out. She rushed into her office, picked up her phone, removed her comfortable flats and stepped into her black boots in the closet. Once she had everything she jogged out to catch the elevator and climbed on.

Daughtrey whistled and directed for more men to come over as he unlocked the cabinet to grab vests. "Ride out behind us. We want two cars at all times in front and behind."

Gregory scrolled on his phone, then raised his head to stare at everyone. "I sent the address we're going."

Teagan grasped the gun and tucked it in her holster.

"Listen up. We have no idea what we're running into. I need you all focused and heads clear. Emily is one of our witnesses from the bus explosion. The priority is to keep her safe."

"Any questions?" Daughtrey shouted.

Teagan turned and jogged to get in the car behind Broderick and Spider. "Be safe out there."

Gregory handed over a small monitor with wired access of Emily's building. She plugged her headset into her ear.

"Keep the channel clear." Teagan rolled her neck left to right.

Each black SUV reversed out of the garage and lined up on the road with them swerving into traffic at higher speeds with sirens on. Teagan prayed they got to Emily in time because situations like this are far too similar to what she's dealt with in the past.

Chapter Eight

T urkey seven years ago.

Teagan pulled the scarf over her hair, held her hands together and scanned the cafe, waiting for her contact to meet at the designated time.

Low voices rambled on and laughter filled the small district. It was a bright and sunny day to get the final info on where a known terrorist group was planning a hit. At only thirty-one, Teagan received orders to take on the role of making contact and establishing a friendship with Lionel Rollins, a retired CIA operative who moved overseas and married. When word spread of him working with a terrorist group, Teagan took the job given to her by the Agency to gain more information.

Lionel held the newspaper in his hand and sat down at the table behind her. "We shouldn't be meeting so out in the opening."

"I had to see you. We heard on phone tap of an attack coming to America."

"From who?"

"Lionel, we're not playing games you know."

"My family and I need to be kept out of whatever you're doing here."

"If you help us, we can keep them protected."

"All I know is they're planning something in a smaller city."

Teagan glanced around the cafe. A few men appeared in the doorway and stared. She lifted her head and caressed her cheek to hide her mouth. "When?"

"Not sure. I couldn't stay long with them."

"The only way we can get you and your family out safely is more information."

Before Teagan had a chance to do anything, loud gunfire engulfed the cafe and she dropped to the ground. She shoved a table in front of her and crawled behind a wall and watched Lionel be killed by multiple bullets.

"Arghhhh!"

Screams and cries of pain filled the surrounding area, as the men ran off and left bodies piled on the floor. A few of her men came in to help secure the location. She sprinted toward Lionel and applied a hand against his neck to feel his pulse and knew he was dead.

"What the hell happened?" Broderick barked at his team.

Teagan stood and wiped her hand clean on her pants. "We need to get out of here. They spotted me."

"Are you hit?" Daughtrey questioned, lifting her chin to gaze into her eyes.

"I'm fine. we have to get to his family."

"Warren's on it already."

"Shit! I forgot about Warren."

"He's pissed, but we have no time to babysit him," Broderick said.

"*That's his friend. Broderick, show some respect,*" *Spider snapped.*

Teagan held a hand to her forehead and exhaled a breath. "I promised him we would get his family to safety."

"*We will. Calm down and let's get you out of here.*"

That day never came and Teagan had to deal with Warren's hateful remarks about the job they did in Turkey. He had to bury his friend and found his family was killed in their home with a sign written on the wall of death to the enemy.

"Teagan, you want to try and call her...Teagan?" Spider nudged her in the shoulder.

"Huh?"

"Zoning out again."

"Are we here?" Teagan ignored his comment.

"Yep, try and call her. I see a car parked outside of her building. To make sure it's one of our guys, we should try and call first."

"Give me a second."

Right as Teagan reached to pick up her phone to dial, she received an incoming call at the same time. "Hello."

"Agent Red, Supervising Agent on duty Milton here. We have a problem."

Teagan tensed, and with a sigh she brushed a hand down her face. "Don't tell me she's dead."

"Sorry to say she is and my men as well," Milton answered.

Teagan jumped out of the car and gestured with her hand to check the block before she ended the call. "Shit, we're coming up there now."

"Did they get to her already?" Daughtrey asked.

She clenched her fist in a ball and raised it to her mouth. "Fuck!" Teagan screamed.

"Calm down, Teagan. You tried your best."

Teagan bent over, her hands on her knees. "I want their fucking heads." She stood and rushed in behind Spider and Daughtrey while some backup ran off to check the security car that sat up front.

They went to her door. It was already open and she scanned the trashed apartment. Emily and her roommate's bodies were laid out with bullet holes in their foreheads.

"Has anyone called the police?"

Milton motioned at his watch and planted a hand in his pocket. "Already on their way. I came on my afternoon shift and found it like this. Nothing has been touched."

"Thanks, Milton."

Milton strode to the back of the apartment. Emily had around the clock protection from the Agency. Something or someone from the inner circle made the choice to take her out for a hefty price.

A few of her team members roamed the area searching for clues, taking pictures while she stood off to the side in thought.

The battle in her mind and heart of how to deal with back to back deaths from witnesses under her care plagued her deeply. A loss this big on her watch would not look good as the director.

"I know you already think it's your fault, but you need to get out of your head and focus." Broderick stood tall next to her.

Teagan gazed at his side profile. "How do you know I was thinking it was my fault?"

"Every time I was in charge on a mission and lost someone I had those same feelings."

"I guess you are a psychic. She was terrified they

would come back and I promised she'd be good under my watch."

"You can't blame yourself. Somebody was watching."

"I agree, but who and why is the question."

"She had a detail which means a log of times when they switch shifts."

Teagan walked over to Emily's body. "True. Hey, Gregory."

Gregory jogged back into the living room. "What's up?"

"Tap into the log entry and find out who came to visit within the last twenty-four. And where is the camera footage from the building?"

As Gregory worked on the footage, the screen showed police cars surrounding the building.

Spider walked in and held the door open for local police. "Their building security is looking into getting the footage to me."

"Agent Teagan Red, nice to meet you. Officer Patterson."

"Mr. Patterson, I know it may seem like we're taking over, but this is a potential witness in a potential attack on U.S. soil."

"What can I do to help?"

"Make sure you talk with the residents and get security footage to us ASAP. We believe something will go down in a day or two."

"From the bus incident?"

"Yes. I'm sorry I can't tell you more than what I know."

"No problem. My men will canvas the area."

Teagan grabbed the device from Gregory. She stared at time stamps of names before she glanced at Patterson.

"Thank you and keep this between us please." Teagan held a hand out toward him.

Broderick and Daughtrey worked in the corner of the room going through the mail, the computer on the desk, and voice messages.

Gregory pointed at the screen Teagan held in her hands. "I see the time logs might have been adjusted."

Teagan cocked her head to the side. "Somebody tampered with them."

"Possibly. I noticed it jumped with a double digit, but then it had the same name one."

"Like it was a mistake to throw us off."

"They really wanted her dead."

Teagan bit her bottom lip and scrolled down the row of names. Nothing seemed to jump out beyond the midnight double up in a row.

Knock, Knock!

Teagan raised her head at the sound of the knocks. "I'm supposed to tell an Agent Red I have the footage." The security guard raised the flash drive in the air.

Daughtrey and Broderick marched toward him, grabbed the device and pulled him inside to take a seat. Teagan ambled to the kitchen table and took a seat next to him as Gregory started up the footage.

"Hello, I'm Agent Red. You must be the Lead Security at the building."

"Travis. Nice to meet you and I've worked here for about five years."

"Travis, what can you tell me about Emily and her roommate?" Teagan played it off on giving him any indication she'd already known Emily and depending on his answers would help pick apart any hints if he was behind her death.

"Emily's been a friend and is kind whenever we see each other. It's crazy someone would hurt her. She doesn't have a bad bone in her body."

"Does she have a significant other? Maybe an angry ex?"

"No, Emily's quiet and reserved. Her roommate is cool."

"Have you looked at the video?"

"Yeah and everything seemed normal to me."

"I will be the judge of that. Gregory is it ready?" Teagan smiled.

Gregory pressed play and everybody came around to watch the video of people coming in and out of the building.

"How many angles do you have?"

"Just the front and back."

"Has anyone tried to wipe the video or edit?"

"Hell, no! My team knows I don't play that."

On screen it replayed the door opening to security walking through. Two people wave at the front desk and go out of frame. Change over happened from yesterday at eight am to seven pm and midnight.

Teagan turned and glared at Travis. "Three shifts change and nothing out of the loop."

"Too clean," Broderick muttered. Everyone faced Travis with a dark glare.

"What are you saying?"

"Travis, you seem like a nice guy, but I think we need to have a real conversation about your future."

"My future?"

"See, I hate liars and you are sitting and lying to my face. I can't help but feel like you doctored this video."

Travis raised out of his seat and Daughtrey pushed him back down.

"Wait a minute. I didn't kill anyone."

"I never said you killed anybody, but the money must have been good enough for you to mess with video evidence. How many times have you changed a time stamp to make a little extra cash?"

"Never!" Travis shouted.

Teagan raised her hand and slammed it down on the table. "Shut up! Because in five minutes I will have your ass hauled off to jail and locked up for accessory to commit a domestic attack."

Travis's eyes ballooned wide at her threat. "No. I promise I had no idea this was going to happen."

"So you admit you changed the video."

Travis dropped his head and burst into tears.

"Travis, I really want you to think clearly about your future. I might help you not get the death penalty," Teagan lied, knowing any domestic terrorist convictions would be sentenced to death.

"Please, I promise I just took a little money to pay some bills."

"I don't care. Tell me the truth. And besides, where you're going bills won't even matter."

"He said he was from the FBI."

Teagan gasped and jumped out of her seat. "Keep going."

"He paid me twenty thousand to change the video and he would sign in normally. I had no reason to question him."

"What's his name?"

"Uhhh... Warren..." Travis wagged a finger in the air. "Agent Warren Johnson."

Gregory clicked while Teagan waved for Daughtrey, Spider, and Broderick to follow down the hallway.

"The FBI agent from the other day that you had words back and forth with," Daughtrey reminded everyone.

"It makes sense it would be him."

"What are you not telling us?"

"From the Turkey mission, he's still holding a grudge." Broderick stared at Teagan.

"That happened years ago and he's still bitching," Daughtrey grunted.

Teagan placed a hand on his shoulder. "Calm down."

"Why do I feel more worried than you?"

"Warren lost someone close to him and I understand the pain." Teagan glanced from Daughtrey to Broderick, thinking back to her friend she lost in Italy.

Spider whispered, looking over his shoulder at the table as Travis talked to Gregory. "Are you sure Travis is telling the truth? I mean he could be throwing out anything to stay out of jail."

"He's not lying, I had a feeling Warren would try and get me back."

"By killing innocent people?" Spider asked.

"It's not about innocent people. It's about making me seem incompetent to hurt my credibility."

Daughtrey dragged a hand down his face and walked off.

"I got something!" Gregory yelled, and everyone ran back to the table.

Gregory shuffled through the frames on the other flash drive Travis handed off and rewound the frames of after midnight with Warren walking through from the front door with his head down avoiding cameras.

"Obviously he knew the camera layout," Spider commented.

Warren walked down the lobby to the security area and flirted with the guard on duty. She walked briefly out of frame and he followed her.

"So he must have gone up and killed the girls. Fast forward," Teagan said.

Ten minutes later he comes back down talking with Travis.

Teagan turned the computer and pointed for Travis to look at him and Warren at the front desk. "So here is where you took the money after he killed an innocent woman."

"I swear he asked to remove him because it was a surprise to set up her bedroom for their anniversary. I never imagined he would kill her." Travis burst into sobs.

"Take him and someone find the woman that was on duty."

Casper and Officer Patterson walked back into the apartment. "No need. We got a body in the alley that matches her description."

All eyes moved to Travis.

Teagan and the team finished up taking inventory of each piece of evidence and talking with the coroner on getting a time of death recorded. Teagan stepped off the elevator. Her eyes trailed up to the high ceilings and back to the door.

"Warren is not answering. They say he's out on call." Spider held up his phone.

"What case is he working on right now?"

"Since we took over the bus one, nothing."

Teagan climbed back in the vehicle. "Find out his hangouts and get back to me as soon as possible, and what do we have on the people that followed us the other night?"

"Should have an update in the hour."

"Time is running out. I want answers."

Spider sat back in the seat next to her and made some calls. Daughtrey turned the ignition and moved into the main lane as Broderick drove in the next truck with Casper and Gregory.

Chapter Nine

That same afternoon, across town Doctor Shrouder rushed back into his office. He shut and locked his door, then sprinted to the desk drawer. He unlocked it and removed the disposable phone and pressed the one button, waiting for the person to answer. Sweat trickled down his forehead, his breathing hitched from lack of sleep and the stress of Angela's death being updated as murder.

"Hello," her sweet voice appeared.

"We need to talk."

"Doctor Shrouder, how are you?"

He lifted the picture of his family on top of his desk, then bit down on his bottom lip nervously. "Megan, I need to see you right away."

"Is something wrong? Why are you whispering?"

Doctor Shrouder dropped his head in disappointment. "Because I got the report back and it says her death certificate is showing murder."

"Relax. I'm not really sure what you're talking about."

Doctor Shrouder's face pulled into confusion. "Have you forgotten you paid me --"

"Hey, shut the fuck up. How do I know you're not recording this call?" Megan investigated.

"What? I wouldn't even know how to do something like that."

"Well, again, I have no idea of what you're implying. My time at the hospital is over and I'm moving on."

"Wait! You have to help me."

"Help you?" Megan chuckled.

"Yes! I doctored those files and left the room so you could do it."

"Tsk tsk, Doctor. I think you've been hitting the bottle too much. How would you like for the board to find out their star surgeon has a drinking and gambling problem?"

He grumbled and fell back in the chair. "I can't lose my legacy."

"You won't as long as you play your part."

He loosened his tie. "When can I see you?"

"Our time is up. This is the last time we will speak to each other."

"What! No I have to see you and touch you."

Megan giggled.

Bang, Bang!

Doctor Shrouder startled at the sudden loud knocks on his door and crouched to the corner of the room. "Who is it?"

"Remember we never spoke," Megan mumbled, then hung up.

"Doctor, Director Teagan Stone. I need to speak with you."

He looked down at his cell, then to the trash bin in the

corner. He stomped on top of his phone and tossed it inside. He angled his glasses upward and adjusted his tie.

Knock, Knock!

"Doctor," Teagan hissed.

He stepped into his bathroom and checked his appearance. "Coming." Finally he walked out and headed to unlock the door and waved them in to take a seat.

"Can I help you, Director Stone?"

"Yes, do you know this woman?" Teagan held a picture of Megan from an arrest photo.

He grasped the photo in his hand. "No, I don't. Should I?"

Teagan watched him closely, his movements fidgety, slow and he constantly swiped sweat from his forehead. "What about this photo?" Teagan flipped the file folder open and removed a picture of Megan in her nurse's uniform.

"That's nurse Bailey."

"Bailey or Megan Rogers?"

"I'm afraid you have me lost, Director Stone."

Teagan tilted her head to the side. "Megan is the person you were just on the phone with, am I correct?"

The doctor peered at the wastebasket and back to Teagan before he dashed toward it, grabbing it at the same time Spider rushed in and pulled him back by the collar of his white coat.

"Daughtrey, hold him!" Spider barked.

"Wait! I can explain," the doctor choked.

"Sit down and tell us how you orchestrated the death of a young woman and the attempted mass murder in a terrorist act."

"Listen. Bailey, I mean, Megan told me it was a simple conversation."

Daughtrey grasped him around the neck. "Stop lying!"

"Daughtrey, we can't kill him in here."

Doctor Shrouder gasped in shock at her statement, then raised his hands up to push Daughtrey back.

"Release him so he can talk."

"Answer her!" Daughtrey spat.

"She was hired like a week ago, at least that's what she told me and I worked a few night shifts with her and we got to talking."

"Keep going."

"She explained she needed to talk to Angela alone because her brother was looking for her after she went missing."

"And you believed her."

"I thought I was helping her."

"Megan used you and Angela's mother had to deal with burying her, along with two other women, and some of my men got killed because of your actions."

"Other women killed?" he muttered.

Teagan slipped photos of Emily and her roommate out and placed them on the desk. "That's Emily and her friend, both killed today by Megan and her friends."

"I -I-" he stuttered.

Teagan stood up and walked around to the side of the desk next to the doctor. "You're sorry. I understand being seduced into thinking a young, beautiful woman could be attracted to you. Probably offered you a blow job during the lunch hour and sex if you covered it up. Am I to assume you got the sex part?"

He lowered his head in shame. "Two nights ago."

"My men and I want to catch Megan before she does

this to another person. Do you have any idea where she's staying?"

"We met at a motel once."

"Write the address down, and a phone number."

"One time I called her from my office line, but mostly on my cell."

Spider tossed the phone in the evidence bag. "Nothing I can salvage."

"The person that came to visit Angela that pretended to be her boyfriend. Can you describe him?"

"I never saw him."

"Well, you're in luck because we got a photo from the hospital entrance. I would suggest getting an attorney, Doctor Shrouder."

Doctor Shrouder extended a hand to stop them from leaving. "What's going to happen to me? I answered your questions."

"Pray we find Megan because otherwise, you're taking the fall, but if we have another explosion and we have mass murder, you won't make it through the night in a cell block."

Teagan snatched the photos and folder, then marched out to the hallway at a frantic pace, trying to compose her anxiety.

Broderick approached. He laid a hand on her back, but she backed up and shook her head.

"Relax. You have to breathe."

"We are two steps behind him."

"He's going to make a mistake."

"Broderick, you know he's been probably planning this for years."

Daughtrey dragged the doctor out in handcuffs and

handed him over to Casper. Gregory and Spider trailed behind him.

Daughtrey held the elevator for Teagan. "Where are we going now?"

"I have to think."

"Warren is still not answering his phone," Spider mentioned.

"Run down everything again for me. Gregory, start off first to help at clearing my head."

Gregory handed his computer to Daughtrey. Everyone in a single line trailed after them to the front entrance of the emergency room.

"Doctor and Megan connected to kill Angela after setting up a car crash with a bus. Two phone calls went out. Emily was told a bomb was going off at the same time or within minutes based on phone records."

Daughtrey slipped keys from his pocket and stood at the passenger side. "Emily gets a weird note, which means someone is working with Megan, because Spider matched her from the protest."

"So she's probably working with the people from the protest," Spider responded.

"They're all connected back to Warren. Payback aimed at me."

"Reasons beyond why he would jeopardize his career to hurt innocent people."

Teagan snapped her finger. "That's it! Hurt innocent people the same way he blamed me for the innocent death of his friend and him never moving on from it is because I was pushed in an elevated role."

"He's stalled," Broderick replied.

"Exactly. The justification is fluid because to him I should have never been given the job in the first place back then, a young woman taking on her third undercover role."

"So you're telling me Warren is jealous of you."

"People do things for all types of reasons, big or small. A man's ego will never be justified."

Teagan rolled the window up at her words, while all the guys' mouths dropped open at her response.

"She's going to kill him," Daughtrey murmured.

"How are we going to explain the death of an FBI agent?" Spider threw his hands in the air.

Gregory raked a hand on the back of his neck. "We can't."

"Shit, when she's pissed anything can happen," Casper said.

Broderick rubbed his cheek and went to his truck. "Oh, I know."

* * *

After hours of sitting outside of Warren's home, Teagan sat back in renewed thought on her early time in the field working undercover. Her life could at most times be dangerous, but often high stakes held a little glamour. Diego being one of them. Warren's rivalry amounted to a one side thing she overlooked and now payment is coming back in the blood of people who are just trying to survive in the world.

Daughtrey passed a cup of coffee back and she cupped it with both hands, then blew over the top to cool it down.

"From his supervisor, Warren hasn't checked in for the last ten hours, probably gone out of the country by now."

"No, he's still here."

"She's right. He wants to see when the big blast happens." Broderick stood outside of the truck.

Gregory finished his call and stepped back over to the van. "That was the Agency. The doctor has been debriefed, along with Travis. They're wondering if we should close the Capitol down for tourists."

"Searches already done?"

"Yeah, and nothing was found."

"Megan's apartment that Doctor Shrouder gave up?"

"Checked and it was clear."

Teagan sat up in her seat as a car drove down the block. All eyes watched the Ford truck slow down and turn at the stop sign at the corner.

"I have a feeling it's happening tomorrow."

Daughtrey withdrew his hands from his pockets. "It might, but it's too late to shut the entire city down."

"Not the entire city, but buses and major locations tourists visit." Teagan attempted to run every lane as a precaution.

"Still not enough time to clear things for blocks." A sense of dread rolled through the pit of Gregory's stomach.

"Blocks, city blocks."

"Maybe call it a night and we try tomorrow," Broderick suggested.

"Have the blueprints on my desk tomorrow morning-" Teagan's phone lit up making her pause. She reached down in her bag to see a call from her husband.

"I have to take this call."

The guys walked off to give her privacy.

"Hey, honey."

"You coming home for dinner?" Christian asked.

"Yes, we're wrapping up now."

"Good. Maybe you can help Cole with his homework." Christian sighed.

Teagan cackled at his comment. "Why am I always given the homework?"

"Because your son doesn't understand the idea of doing homework right when he gets off from school. Drives me nuts."

"Sorry but that's your son. I remember you did the same back thing in school."

"Anyway, dinner will be ready soon."

Teagan peered at Warren's home and frowned. "Okay, love you."

"To the moon and back," Christian replied.

Teagan gulped the rest of her coffee and waved for everybody to get back in the car. "I have a headache, and my kid needs help with his homework."

"We're leaving his place with no backup."

"Casper and Broderick can stay and report back in the morning."

"Gotcha, Boss." Casper gestured to the driver's side and Broderick jumped in the passenger seat.

Daughtrey turned the key and drove down the street to take Teagan home.

"Spider, have another call come out, and you guys meet in the morning at the Capitol."

"Police will ask questions."

"Make sure to update each federal and local agency. We can't have a panic, but if something is happening, they need to be aware."

Teagan arrived back home to her family filled with comfort of joy and laughter at the reason why she continues to do her job with the Agency.

Chapter Ten

D*ay of Event*

Perry, Samson, and Megan packed up the guns, ammunition, and supplies tucked in the compartments of the camouflaged floral van he'd stolen to use as cover. Early morning at four am, they'd showered and dressed, prepared for war. Megan pushed her hair into a black headband, then put on a black jumpsuit. All day long yesterday they talked over plans, continued to run it down on how things would happen. And after learning of Emily's death by Warren, everything shifted it into faster gear. They would finally make everything happen on their end to blow up their target in less than two hours. Samson hopped in the front seat next to Perry and placed ear monitors and walkies on to keep track. Perry double checked his pockets for his ID badge to get through the gate.

Megan stood next to him with a wide grin on her face and pecked him on the mouth.

"Are you ready to do it? No turning back now."

"I have everything under control. You make sure to be ready with your performance for the audience."

Megan giggled and stood on her tippytoes and grasped his shirt, giving him a lingering kiss. Samson honked the horn causing them to pull apart.

"I can't wait to get rid of him," Megan hissed and flipped him off.

Perry cupped her chin and pecked her on the lips. "Be nice. We're a team."

"I know."

"He has to run the play and you follow his move."

"We are locked in, Perry. Nothing can go wrong."

Perry walked around to Samson and checked in. "Remember once they figure out the fake bomb, we need to hit it at the correct time."

"Sooner we leave the better."

"Warren will send the final payment when he hears confirmation."

"He should have paid us up front for the type of job we're doing and the risks."

"I have a backup plan if he stalls."

"What is your plan?"

"We won't be the only ones going down. Head out and I will follow behind and we break off one on the block."

Perry balled his fist and knocked on the top of the car to go. He jogged to the van and hopped in and sped behind them. Less than twenty minutes later, they arrived before six in the morning with the slow trail of cars commuting. Samson and Megan idled by a few blocks while watching as Perry pulled up to the gate and showed his ID for the gardening service that was scheduled.

"He's got less than one hour to be in and out before we start."

"Perry knows what to do. If he gets caught, it's on him, but we stick to blowing it up even on our end."

"Just hope he gets out in time."

Samson planted a hand on Megan's thigh and squeezed. "Why? Because you'll miss him?" He grasped her chin, pulled her face forward and pressed a kiss on her lips. Megan moaned and shoved him back with her hand raised to slap him across the face.

"I told you we're done."

"We are done when I say we're done."

"Perry will kill you for touching me."

Samson snatched her arm, then shoved her to his chest. "Bitch, remember who brought you in on making this money."

Megan grinned, slid her tongue across her lips and ran her hand up his chest. "I'm sorry, baby."

"You should be. Watch your mouth."

"Perry thinks we will be together and I tried to play it off."

"The minute we finish here, we can take him out."

"Oh, I love that idea."

"Look, he's driving through." Samson tapped her on the leg, motioned to the gate opening and Perry driving forward.

Megan reached for the signs in the back of the van and noticed a group of protestors lining up out front of the White House.

"Showtime," Megan said. She unzipped her jacket and removed her ponytail to let her hair fall around her face and checked her makeup.

"Remember once the time hits six we start," Samson reminded her.

Megan and Samson got out of the vehicle, sauntered to the group of protestors and blended in with their signs.

Perry on the other side of the gate introduced himself to the other team of workers on duty and eyed the security team walking back and forth.

"How much you bet we will be here all day because of those damn protestors," a middle height, dark low-cut hair, stalky guard yammered on.

"They do this every day?" Perry investigated, removed his tools and stood next to the bushes of trees.

"No, only for the past week, but I'm ready to lock them all up," the grumpy guard mumbled.

Perry chuckled and bent at the knee. He pulled out a few shovels and a weed cutter and laid them beside him. As soon as the guard turned his back and stalked off toward the base haul of the guard gate, Perry whipped around and unscrewed the drain in the right corner. No cameras were located. He unzipped his bag and placed the first explosive inside slowly, as a dry breeze wafted in the air. A few people started to walk in his direction. Perry quickly moved back in his original spot and dug up more dirt to pull weeds into a trash bag. Bright, shiny sunlight beamed down, but it became blocked when the caretaker approached on a go-cart.

"Normally we have the first breaks around an hour and a half. Some of us go grab coffee together if you're interested," he suggested, then sat back with a straw hat on his head.

Perry peered from the ground up into his face and smiled. "Sounds good, but I might pass. I have another job afterwards. The boss is raging on me to hurry up."

He shrugged. "Suit yourself. You'll miss all the good donuts," he responded, then started the cart up, made a U-turn and went back to the opposite end to enter the employee area. Perry let out a breath, rubbed his forehead free from sweat and moved further around the corner to another drain hole and started to add another bomb.

"Last one and then we're ready to go," he mumbled to himself.

Loud voices across the street blasted away from a group of protesters letting him know Megan and Samson were in place.

"Almost time." Perry grinned.

* * *

Teagan shoved the gate closed and stared out at the team of agents ready to go out into the field. Another mission was upon her to make sure each one came home safe to their families on top of saving the innocent lives of Americans. The bodies of the security team who were killed by Warren, and Emily's death, stayed on her mind for the past twenty-four hours.

"Aye! Shut up so we can hear!" Daughtrey shouted, then he nodded at Teagan to begin.

Teagan raised her hand and scratched her nose. "I have to say this every time, and I mean it because we are family. When we leave these walls our goal is the same-- protect the innocent and take out whatever gets in our way."

The crowd started to clap hands.

"That feels harsh, not the proper thing to say as agents, but again we are a special group, an elite group. I look into your eyes and know you have my back and I have yours." Teagan gazed into their eyes, one by one.

"We got you, Boss!" Casper yelled, making a few chuckle.

Teagan smiled back. "Thank you, Casper. We have a team moving now on the U.S. Capitol to sweep it for any suspicious packages, and everybody is being screened." Teagan cleared her throat. "Plus, we have a list going around with photos of the suspects, Gregory has obtained."

Spider cocked his chin up in the air and gestured time to go.

"Any questions?"

"Triple check your gear, vests, headsets. No one goes anywhere alone," Spider demanded.

"Let's ride out." Teagan ambled to the passenger seat of the black SUV.

Broderick hopped in to drive. Daughtrey and Casper sat in the back with guns locked and loaded.

A fleet of trucks piled out of the Agency, speeding down the road, Teagan's phone vibrated with the latest news report.

"Breaking story of the death of the young woman from the car accident was tied to a bomb explosion. This is based on a call in tip we have yet to verify, but we will keep you updated," the news anchor expressed.

Teagan groaned and dialed Albert at the White House to put the rumors to rest, to stop the spread of misinformation as they were arriving to their destination.

"The president is pissed. I have back to back calls from other Congress members all over the news."

"Get a press release out that we are on top of everything, and nothing is confirmed."

"The Press Secretary will make a statement. Any updates on finding them?"

"Not yet. Warren never came back home, and we checked out the apartment with no luck."

Teagan looked out of the window. "Thanks, Albert. We're almost at the Capitol now." She raised her wrist to check the time. "Coming up on almost seven am."

"Alright Teagan, I will stall as much as possible."

Daughtrey tapped her on the shoulder, and she ended the call. "Check out the protestors."

As she scanned the growing crowd, her throat tightened at the possibility of one of them working with the enemy.

Spider stuck his head out of the window. "Too many people out here to cover. We might have to redirect traffic."

They slowly came to a stop and parked at the corner of the street a few steps from the light before making it to the Capitol and climbing from the back.

Daughtrey looked around with narrowed eyes at people walking back and forth in groups. A few staff members were turned away.

Teagan picked up her walkie and stood next to him. "Gregory, get me eyes on every entrance and exit. We're about to head in now."

"Check your phone now. Just sent the link from the drone," Gregory responded.

Broderick waved a hand in the air to move the crowd back from coming further.

"Why do I feel like it's going too easy?"

"What do you mean?"

She held a hand up and covered her eyes to block out

the sun. "Too quiet. Nothing out of place, no pushback or disruption."

Two Agency team members ran down the steps toward her and Daughtrey and removed their helmets. "Agent Stone, nothing is here."

"You searched every square inch."

"Yes, we doubled up on staffing. Each office and trash bin were searched."

"A false alarm." Daughtrey's face scrunched up.

Teagan tapped her hand against her thigh. "Why set us up on a false alarm?"

"Warren was playing us."

"Warren put us on a false chase to get us here, to keep us from the target."

"What's more important than the U.S. Capitol? It's not like they can get to the president," a younger agent who was clean-shaven with an athletic build and light brown skin answered.

Daughtrey and Teagan whipped their heads around at his comment. "The White House!"

Teagan rushed to dial Albert back while running down the stairs to jump back in the car. "Fuck, pick up Albert," she mumbled, wiped the sweat off her brow.

"Let's go!" Daughtrey shouted. Broderick, Gregory, and Spider turned and sprinted back to the truck.

"What happened?" Gregory squinted in confusion.

"False chase. We have to get to the president."

"What about here?"

"This was a hoax to throw us off. Daughtrey, get us to the White House. I don't care about running lights."

Broderick, along with Gregory, started to pick up their phones and make calls. "Shit, that would play around the world, and make our enemies look at us as open to more hits."

Daughtrey pushed the gas to the hilt, turned down the road speeding past buses and cars as they honked and cursed at him.

"Albert! Code Red."

"He's in a meeting. I need to get the chief of staff on the line, the vice president is out of the country."

"Whatever you do, make sure the press is blocked out. We can't have this getting released."

"Teagan."

"I know, Albert. Just stay calm. The less chaos the better. We have no reason to think they're going to set it off yet. They still think we're searching the Capitol."

At a swift turn, Daughtrey almost collided with a school bus and slammed on the brakes. He backed up and shifted gears and whipped around to the left. He passed by Ford's theater and made it to Pennsylvania Avenue. Teagan barely waited for the car to stop when she jumped out. It made security pull their guns as she raised her hands, her eyes darted around the street.

"Keep your hands in the air!"

"We're on the same side. I need the president moved now."

Spider and Gregory came over with their badges held out. "You must be new here, but we're with the Agency and she's Director Teagan Stone."

"Agent Red," the young security guard muttered.

Teagan snatched the walkie out of his hand. "Code Red, I repeat Code Red." She released a breath.

"Oh shit." Spider took off running, causing Daughtrey and Gregory to follow.

"Broderick, follow me. Casper, take two teams and get the bomb team here." Teagan snatched her gun holster and jogged up the hill as more men came out of the White House, they got Albert and the president, along with the chief of staff shoved into the limo.

Teagan chucked her chin up at Albert in recognition, swerved around the barrier and sprinted up to a few employees being lined up.

"Search them for weapons," Broderick demanded, then tapped a guard to keep moving in front of him.

Out the corner of her eye Teagan saw a man bent down near the garden packing a bag. He lifted his shoulder and he made eye contact with her.

"Freeze!" Teagan shouted.

Perry smiled. "Warren said you would figure it out."

"Put the bag down."

Broderick walked to the opposite side of Teagan with his gun pointed at Perry.

"Too late."

Teagan stalked forward. "It's never too late, to stop."

"Come any closer and I'll set them off."

"The president's gone. You've done all this for nothing."

"Burn it down! Burn it down! Government is lying!" Shouts and screams from protestors continued to get louder.

"Let me go! Perry!"

Teagan glanced at Spider handcuffing a woman. "Perry, are you sure about killing innocent people?"

Perry's voice made her spine stiffen with emotion. "If the money is right."

"Hopefully it was worth every penny." Teagan rolled

her neck and a red dot appeared pointed at Perry's forehead and the shot was taken.

"No!" Megan screamed and tried to break free of Spider.

They rushed to the dead body and slid his bag away gently. Teagan bent down, lugged the bag in front of her and unzipped it slowly. She looked at the pile of material for gardening and guns inside.

"Guys, get the place completely cleared. From his gear it could be buried around here somewhere."

"Teagan! Teagan! We got him."

"Who?"

"Warren, the girl blabbed that he's on his way to the train station." Gregory shoved his phone toward her to take.

A cameo shot of Warren buying a ticket.

"He's on his way to the police station."

"Hold him in a cell with a few people that aren't so nice about being blown up." The Teagan they were used to was by the book ninety percent of the time, but her ice cold interior was slowly showing on the outside.

Broderick's left brow hiked up at her words.

"You got it."

"Is that wise to do?"

"Being wise in this moment is what I should be, but I can ask for forgiveness later."

Pop!

"Teagan, get down!"

"Are you hit?"

Pop!

Everyone drew their guns shooting back at Samson running away from the protestors. Daughtrey dashed off and leaped, clapping a hand down on his shoulders making Samson lose the gun. The crowds watched, filming on their cells at the incident. An ambulance pulled up, along with more police.

Teagan gripped her shoulder, slowly winched in pain, eyes drawing closed. The EMT jogged over to help right when she fainted in Broderick's arms.

Epilogue

Christian walked in the hospital holding a bag of food. He watched Teagan stare at the same news report of the president being driven out of the White House to avoid another terrorist plot. Teagan smiled and sat up in the bed and cupped his chin and pecked his lips.

"I am starving." A feeling of excitement stirred in the pit of her stomach.

"How are you feeling?"

Her eyes lifted to meet his. "Better. Ready to go home and sleep in my own bed."

"Had me worried."

"Me too, but the doctors got the bullets out. No real harm done," she said, swallowing the lump in her throat.

"The kids are ready for you to come home. Tatum keeps trying to come up here."

"I know. I talked to her last night and she kept crying about coming with you today."

"So, Warren was arrested and the woman, Megan?" A mask of reserve seemed to cover his face.

"Yeah. Crazy to think a person you've worked with in the past is responsible for something that could have killed a lot of people."

Christian raked a hand down her arm, then up her neck.

"I missed real food."

Christian chuckled and slid in on the edge of the bed. "Where did all these flowers come from?"

"The guys."

"Tell them slow their roll, making me look bad."

Teagan smirked. "Please, you know you're the only one."

"Good news is you're coming home tomorrow."

She wiped her hand on his napkin and gulped her sweet tea. "Did you tell the kids?"

Christian nodded and picked up her trash and tossed in the bin next to the bed.

"Oh, turn it up."

"My fellow Americans, it is in moments where we come together and give thanks for the wonderful work our law enforcement continues to do in order to protect us," the president said.

"I forgot to call Albert back."

"First and foremost, I want to give my prayers and well wishes to Agent Teagan Stone on a speedy recovery," the president mentioned.

Christian laid a hand on her thigh in comfort, and Teagan interlocked their hands.

"The people responsible for this plan are apprehended or dead. All explosives have been recovered and together new protocols will be implemented over the next few weeks," the president explained.

Christian stretched a hand to grab the remote and

turn the TV off. The door opened with a few of her team members walking in with balloons and teddy bears.

"Boss Lady is finally up." Daughtrey grinned and shook hands with Christian.

"I could have sworn I told all of you to stop buying me gifts."

"See, I knew we could have just spent some money on food and she wouldn't notice," Casper joked.

Daughtrey glared at him.

"Shut up, Casper!" everyone yelled.

Teagan fluffed her pillow. "How are things while I'm gone?" She pointed at the empty seats.

Daughtrey looked up at the TV screen. "Good. Broderick is leading the briefs and Gregory is monitoring Warren's progress."

"Spider, are you the lead on his interrogation?"

"Yep and he's already pleaded guilty," Spider replied.

She pinched her lower lip with her teeth. "Good, I hope they throw the book at him."

"Glad to see you looking better," Spider said.

Their continued conversation was interrupted by the nurse who came in holding a tray of medicine. She handed it off to Teagan, grabbed the clipboard off the wall and monitored her stats.

"I will be back at the office soon."

"Not too soon, right, nurse?" Christian winked at her.

"Right, you have to take it easy, Mrs. Stone," Nurse Glenda answered.

"Boss man laying the law down," Daughtrey teased.

Teagan rolled her eyes. "Anyway, thanks for checking up on me guys, but I need to get sleep." Teagan pulled the blanket up to her neck.

Spider turned and hugged Teagan goodbye, then

Daughtrey marched out of her room as Christian sat back on the couch in the corner.

Teagan yawned and cupped her mouth. "How mad will you be if I go confront Warren?"

Christian tilted his head, his face balled up in a frown. "Why are you thinking about Warren? Let the team handle him."

"One conversation."

Christian scrubbed a hand down his face. "No way to stop you if I say I am against your decision?"

"I won't be alone with him."

"That's all I can ask for."

* * *

Silence in the room enclosed her thoughts as she waited for him to enter, with her arm in a sling, Teagan waited to rest up more with her family before deciding to come to and talk with Warren. Christian stood in the corner next to Spider, waiting in anticipation to end her presence around the prison. The red dot turned on making them aware a prisoner was about to enter. Mirrors held cameras that were turned on recording the talk.

"Director Stone, you have a few minutes with him."

"I only need five."

Warren smirked and slouched down in the chair, his hands locked to the table.

"Looks like you've been in a few fights."

The smile fell from his face. He grunted and peered at the extra security in the corner against the wall. The only way for him to stay alive was to be under lockdown twenty-three hours a day except for shower time.

"I came here to find out where it went wrong,

Warren. I mean, a long time FBI agent doesn't go rogue to the point of committing a crime to kill hundreds of people in an attack on the president."

He grunted.

She lifted her right arm in the sling. "This will heal, but you will spend the rest of your life in prison, while I go on with my life to see my kids grow old, and be blessed to become a grandmother."

"All of it was your fault. You should have listened to me."

"I did my job."

"Because of you I almost was killed last night."

She shrugged, then pushed up in the chair. "They should have tried harder."

Christian started to move toward her and she raised a hand to stop him.

"My goal was to kill enough people to show how incompetent the president and the Agency is when domestic attacks happen. Unfortunately people I paid to do the job fucked up. But next time I won't miss."

"Warren, I made mistakes when I was younger, including not having backup do a sweep of the cafe that day, but we all knew the risks that we all signed up for when we pledged to give our lives to the cause. Now I can be your worst nightmare. A few bullets will never stop me. Next time, come harder when trying to play these games."

* * *

I hope you enjoyed Teagan's story so far. Please also check out "**Agent Red (Mission) Teagan Stone Book 10**" coming soon.

Also, if you love Mystery, Suspense check out "**Mirror of Lies Book 1**" https://books2read.com/u/mgjEPx

Another thriller, crime fiction "**Ruined Book 1**" https://books2read.com/u/bzVGAj

Check out a free short here: *"The Firm"* https://payhip.com/b/py7S

Grab Boxset "**Agent Red 1-3**" here https://payhip.com/b/1KcxY

Teagan Stone Reading Order of Series

1.Agent Red—Fatal Memory Book 1
https://books2read.com/u/4j2PYX
2.Agent Red—Fatal Target Book 2
https://books2read.com/u/bWP8Jq
3.Agent Red—Fatal Crime Book 3
https://books2read.com/u/mZadZJ
4.Agent Red—Fatal Justice Book 4
https://books2read.com/u/mq07wd
5.Agent Red—Fatal Enemy Book 5
https://books2read.com/u/bxe01q
6. Agent Red—Fatal Death Book 6
https://books2read.com/u/mqwlRv
7. Agent Red—Fatal Revenge Book 7
https://books2read.com/u/3JnKyA
8. Agent Red—Fatal Pursuit Book 8
https://books2read.com/u/bOPow0
9. Agent Red—Fatal Attack Book 9
https://books2read.com/u/bwwKWP
10. Agent Red—Fatal Mission Book 10

Reading Order of Mirror Series

Mirror of Lies Book 1
https://books2read.com/u/mgjEPx

Mirror of Lust Book 2
https://books2read.com/u/mVRpz2

Mirror of Danger Book 3
https://books2read.com/u/b5z8o1

Mirror of Murder Book 4

Mirror of Escape Book 5

Acknowledgments

I want to thank my team, who helps me behind the scenes, from my editors to my test readers and graphic designers, and the list goes on. I truly appreciate each of you for keeping me on my toes.

About the Author

Ava S. King is the debut author of thriller, mystery, suspense, and psychological crime novels.

If you want to know when the next book will come out, please visit Author Ava S. King website at http://www.authoravasking.com, where you can sign up to receive an email for her next release.

What's Next?

Want to know what happens next? Follow me at the links below to catch the next release.

Thank you so much for reading, and if you enjoyed the crazy ride and decided to leave a review, we'd truly appreciate the support. Reviews are the lifeblood of the publishing world. They're read, appreciated, and needed. Please consider taking the time to leave a few words on Goodreads or BookBub.

Sign up for updates and sneak peeks at the sites below:

www.authoravasking.com
www.bookbub.com/avasking
www.goodreads.com/author/avasking
www.Twitter.com/authoravaking
www.Instagram.com/authoravasking
www.Facebook.com/authoravasking
www.304publishing.tumblr.com

About 304 Publishing Company

We showcase authors writing African American, interracial, women's fiction, urban romance, erotica, and contemporary romance novels, along with thrillers, suspense novels, poetry collections, and beauty & style books.www.304publishing.com

Join our mailing list to stay updated with new releases and blog posts.

www.ingramcontent.com/pod-product-compliance
Lightning Source LLC
Chambersburg PA
CBHW070514200726
48293CB00007B/2524